SKELMERSDALE

D0533222

FICTION RESERVE STOCK
LL 60

Michael Martin lives in the New Forest with his wife and two sons. He left Swansea University halfway through the English course in pursuit of reality, which has so far eluded him. In his search for higher things he has spent much time up on the roofs of old buildings, re-roofing them in traditional materials to preserve their character.

The original of this diary was discovered by him, printed on an unknown metal, discarded by a Wiltshire corn circle. Believing it to contain the wisdom of an advanced civilization, he began to translate it but carried on anyway and completed the translation.

A YEAR NEAR PROXIMA CENTAURI

Michael Martin

CORGI BOOKS

A YEAR NEAR PROXIMA CENTAURI
A CORGI BOOK   055 2 99527 4

First publication in Great Britain

PRINTING HISTORY
Corgi edition published 1992

Copyright © Michael Martin 1992

Text illustrations by Lucy Martin

The right of Michael Martin to be identified as the author
of this work has been asserted in accordance with sections
77 and 78 of the Copyright Designs and Patents Act 1988.

Set in 11/13 pt Compugraphic Cheltenham by
Colset Pte Ltd., Singapore

055541845

Corgi Books are published by Transworld Publishers Ltd,
61–63 Uxbridge Road, London W5 5SA, in Australia by
Transworld Publishers (Australia) Pty Ltd, 15–23 Helles
Avenue, Moorebank, NSW 2170, and in New Zealand by
Transworld Publishers (NZ) Ltd, 3 William Pickering
Drive, Albany, Auckland.

Made and printed in Great Britain by
Cox & Wyman Ltd, Reading, Berks.

To Joseph and Robin

What about a quotation? I thought a quote from
the underrated poet Montague Blyte (1615–1644)
might be appropriate, from his masterwork *Astra
Castra, numen lumen.*

This wonder lyfe hath surely sprung
From fuller founts than oure poore worlde?

JANUARY

My wife and I had not eaten for nearly an hour. I walked into the food store and hacked with relish at an enormous leg of meat which hung on the appropriate spike in the sparkling icy gloom. I took four generous slices, added some purple Ormerloon peppers, a tiny pinch of Gormandine and let them sizzle in the old traditional Gaga we had bought from a little creature in the village. Just as they were greening to perfection I uncorked a bottle of 21634 Halmatrope. We always used to open our bottles three hours before a meal, but the locals tell us that five minutes is adequate and they should know. I placed the opened bottle on the preparation surface next to the bubbling Gaga and I could hear it sucking in the atmosphere. 'Let it hyperventilate for five minutes,' old Mr Dobson, the neighbouring Drool, had told us, 'then, quick as you can, wring its neck and squeeze it into the glass.'

For many years my wife and I had holidayed on this tiny little unspoilt planet. I shall not divulge its name in case you all want to visit us, the sudden shock of which could easily disturb its delicate orbit and send it hurtling into the sun. I am sure I need not remind you of the fate of Pontius B, when two galacto transporter loads of Third Age 'Last Holiday of a Lifetime' travellers landed and disembarked on the same polar cap. The planet instantly tilted on its axis and flew out of its orbit across the paths of the twelve inner planets, neatly popping each one into their sun before it flew off into space. As if that were not tragic enough in itself, it gave the Big Planet Hunters the idea for a whole new sport. Therefore, I am sure you will understand why I shall refer to this planet only as 'Provender'.

When my wife and I decided, for many reasons, that a change of planet and a change of life was needed this was the first place we thought of, with its unspoilt creatures, natural surroundings, interesting and sometimes marvellous weather and, above all, its food and drink.

Everything that lives on Provender can be eaten or drunk without ill effect and most of the living creatures taste superb and respond wonderfully to creative mixing, subtle blending and diverse culinary technique. If something black and hairy you have never seen before scuttles from out of your boot, herd it into a box, give it a puff of Instamort spray, grill it gently in Smolene fat for fifteen minutes, dice it – if its appearance is too offputting – and gulp it down; it's bound to be delicious. One unfortunate discovery we made here by accident many years ago was that the more intelligent the creature the better it tastes. We inadvertently ate the hotel proprietor's great-grandmother before she had had a chance to pass on her arcane knowledge to the next of kin. We had no idea then that their species shrinks and changes colour so alarmingly with age. Now we are more careful, generally, but she was quite the most exquisite morsel my wife and I have ever had; marinaded in a fine old Halmatrope and eaten on a slice of toast rubbed with the flesh of a ripe Sprillet.

Sometimes, as we float on our small lagoon, a fine vintage Algarglanon sprawled in our palms, watching the sky shimmer with rainbows of plasma as the sun hurtles towards the horizon, we look to the approximate position of our home planet Conima and sigh. We just sigh. We sigh for the remorselessly hectic pace of the life we have left, we sigh for the accelerating boundaries of knowledge that we are avoiding, we sigh for the uncontrollable, unforeseen devastation that results from the knowledge that has been acquired far too quickly for anybody to grasp its implications, we just sigh because we have eaten so much that anything more would deplete our last reserves of energy.

One evening, as a light breeze blew us across the lagoon to our patio, I noticed our neighbour, old Mr Dobson, beckoning us with all his arms. I waved back and my wife set the sail on our floating chair to catch the breeze more effectively. Mr Dobson greeted us in the complex, rather embarrassing language of the Drools. The Drools have a perineal larynx making their language hard to master by creatures with a more sensibly placed larynx. However, my wife proved surprisingly adept at the language and was soon able to master the subtle inflections and thus fill the gaps that my faltering grasp left.

Mr Dobson gesticulated at the quivering mountains that surrounded our modest dwelling. It was some time before my wife and I had grasped that these ranges of peculiar vibrating foliage that we had purchased with our house were, in fact, the main foodstuff of the Halmatrope and were harvested at the end of August by means of letting loose clouds of tiny Halmatrope spores on to the crop. These eat voraciously and as soon as they have grown big enough squads of pickers round them up and bottle them. Once in the bottle the Halmatrope grows until its head stoppers itself. It then relaxes into a state of suspended animation until released for consumption, then, as previously described, five minutes of hyperventilation and it is ready. It appeared that Mr Dobson had in fact planted, tended and harvested this crop on an informal basis with the previous owner in return for a share of the Halmatrope. I saw no reason not to continue this salutary practice and I attempted to communicate as much to Mr Dobson, but my wife had to correct me more than once. He scuttled off and was soon back with his arms full of bottles as a gesture to launch our future association. I wondered in passing what Drools tasted like. Mr Dobson shared a bottle with us and left gesticulating wildly as only a Drool can do. I felt that he had accepted us already, but our other neighbours further down the valley might not prove so amenable.

Mr Skeg, who lived alone in a tiny cabin, was a pure blooded Colwig descended from one of the earliest tribes to settle on the planet. It was rumoured that on cold winters nights Colwigs would start to eat themselves, rapidly regenerating in the spring. We had not seen very much of Mr Skeg, just the upper thorax and a head in the distance; perhaps that was why. We resolved to postpone our first neighbourly visit to Mr Skeg's cabin until the spring – late spring.

Beyond Mr Skeg lived five creatures of indeterminate age and species. I speculated in the way one does about neighbours who keep themselves to themselves that they were probably a sort of mongrel variation of Montalbans, in which case, as the Montalbans have five sexes, this was probably as near to the perfect Montalban marriage as was statistically likely for such unprepossessing and antisocial creatures. Now and again we would hear shrieks and wails down the valley and catch a glimpse of one being chased off by four, or two by three, but generally they seemed to stay indoors and emit a sort of low vibration hum, rather like an enormous Capricep purring. Mr Dobson said they never seemed to eat anything, so we have yet to officially introduce ourselves to them. He had himself heard a rumour that they reproduced at an alarming rate and this provided their nutrition, but I never take any notice of rumours, I just repeat them.

We were beginning to think that the brief but extreme Provender winter we had been told about was a rumour as we drifted aimlessly across the lagoon sipping at our half-full glasses, when a strange feeling came over us, a shiver of premonition, or, more likely, a sudden change in the electro-magnetic field. My wife ran up the spinnaker and we made it to the patio pontoon, just as a sheet of green vapour swept down the valley freezing everything in its path. We hid in the summerhouse until it had passed and then slithered and slid over to the house as quickly as we could before the next one came, which proved to be a wise decision.

For the next three days the vapour spiralled and zig-zagged back and forth along the valley. We stayed in. Fortunately we had ample provisions to survive even the worst winter, with additional allowances in case we had to share our provisions with any voracious guests. As we snuggled together in front of a roaring fire, eating and drinking, it occurred to me that the house was not really big enough, at the rate we were growing, and if fate had conspired to trap us for the winter with the last of our summer guests we would all be feeling rather claustrophobic. Also, a roaring fire was all very nice, but as the only form of heating for what was becoming a remarkably cold house, it was not adequate. Something was required with a little less conspicuous noise and rather more widespread heat. I resolved to contact the builders and a plumber as soon as the weather improved.

The buildings of Provender are a joy in themselves after the dreadful monotony of Conima. Creatures with natural advantages adopt a trade or craft that the families seem to continue for generations. Naturally occurring elements are wrested, with the minimum of fuss, from their locations, transported, shaped, if necessary, by the appropriate creature, and added to a structure whose design the customer and builders, in varying proportions, have some say in; unlike the processes on Conima, where vast numbers of genetically engineered molluscs construct specific structures in a sort of coralline material. My wife and I still shudder at the memory of the self-replicating organic hypermarket strain that went haywire and caused enormous identical hypermarkets to spring up overnight all over the country-side, with no consideration of customer demand.

Our house was typical of the area, constructed by the distant ancestor of our local builder, Henry, from enormous lumps of the local rock, using the colossal strength that this particularly squat muscular creature has. My wife and I

hoped that Henry would be able to match the subtle colouring and robust disregard for symmetry that so individual-
ized his great-grandfather's work.

The local stone was, I am told, formed when ancient earth
movements and volcanic activity heated and compressed
the massive accumulation of shed Couth skins. The Couth is
long since extinct, but now and again entire Couth skins are
unearthed, miraculously unscathed by the trials of time,
revealing the unerring eye for detail and tidy stitchwork
which led it to be regarded as the most fashion-conscious
and fastidious of primeval creatures, never allowing itself to
be seen twice by another creature in the same skin. Unfortunately, as the population grew, the poor, vain creatures
refused to adapt, and most died of exhaustion, mid-skin, or
died with no issue, crestfallen, depressed, hidden from
chance inspection. Tragic as this may be, the rock which
evolved is durable, easily worked and will polish up beautifully if desired, revealing hidden folds, pleats, nips and
tucks, trapped in rock for ever, boldly resisting the cruel
arbiter of fashion.

The multiplicity of species on the planet meant that all
speculative construction had to be simple and adaptable to
the general needs of most species. We have a large dining
room and a comfortable spacious sitting room, each with an
open fireplace. The low calorific content of the local timber
and the high proportion of Noxule gas in the atmosphere
conspire to make Provender fires loud, colourful events
rather than particularly warming ones. We also have the
customary broad kitchen with its variety of tools and equipment suitable for dismembering and preparing even the
largest of natural creatures, should the need arise; with the
traditional icy store room attached. There are three bed-
rooms, we are planning two more, and a particularly
resourceful reproduction and gratification suite, equipped
to cater for the subtle climatic, emotional and physical
requirements of any creature we are ever likely to welcome

under our roof. We do have a couple of old friends who are Chrysms, but although we pride ourselves on our liberal attitudes, my wife and I have always insisted that if ever they stay with us they can bring their own Yumice. Last, but not least, the abluting suite. This was something else that would have to be upgraded to our requirements when the weather was more clement. The previous incumbent obviously never washed anything he could not see and with his failing eyesight in the last years this must have precluded virtually everything, necessitating a complete fibril blast of the house before we moved in.

After our three days trapped watching the antics of the green vapour we were a little wary of venturing out. The last of the vapour had rushed off down the valley as unexpectedly as it had come. We had it on good authority that such storms were sudden and infrequent, so, after confining our movements to the immediate vicinity of the house for a few more days, my wife and I bravely resolved to venture out for a meal to an establishment warmly recommended by Mr Dobson, at least my wife was sure that his recommendation was warm.

I unlocked the garage and my Stromba eased itself out into the cool air. I had had misgivings about parting with my prize Ferenziculo when we moved to Provender. When you are accustomed to the best it is hard to settle for anything less: the sleek almost weightless shell, with its frictionless coating, the seats that mould themselves to you and clasp you like an ardent lover and the reflex controls that get you there almost before you have decided where to go. But as Carlo, my Plasmatist on Conima, advised, 'Provender has only two coordinate cells, is three light years from the nearest Plasmatist (ten from the nearest recommended one), and are you going to bring it back to Conima every time it runs out of 41K?' I was convinced: we would have to buy one of Provender's durable, one tries to avoid saying laughable, little Strombas. However, that proved almost as much of a problem as importing a Ferenziculo.

Provender is a gustatory paradise, not a technological one. Anything which does not naturally occur on Provender is regarded as a threat to the economy and the limited ability of the population. In spite of stringent trade policies within the nebula and grant-aid to encourage the importation and adoption of technology established for millennia elsewhere, the inhabitants of Provender continue to tread their own path, which in many areas is preferable to handling a Stromba.

My wife and I had presented ourselves to the nearest Stromba dealer, a young Drool with an annoying turn of phrase. He was not the first dealer we had suspected of speaking perinealy but the first we had met who literally did so. He obviously had never met Conimunculi before, or else had scant regard for their comfort. The first Stromba we tried had no space whatsoever for my wife. In the end we settled for a modified Stromba that had been intended for a Nullion, but he was eaten unexpectedly before collecting it. We said we would have it and could we take it? Apparently not. We had the money, codes of reference, incubation receipts, synaptic verification, even by chance my wife's Scanplan, but no, he wanted more. Could we show our current Species Rating? I said no. 'No Stromba,' he said, squatting for inflection.

I did not need my wife to translate. I have always held the Species Rating in disregard. Actuarial tables of species risk, covering as they do the 7,463 species requiring equipment to transport them, are totally inaccurate. They take no stock of individual aptitude and accomplishment, and only a very general account of environment. It is pure chance that Conimunculi score so low on this scale: the figures were completely distorted thirty years ago when freak interference waves from deep space briefly reversed the controls

18

on every vehicle of the western land masses of Conima, resulting in an average of one accident for every three Conimunculi; every stationary vehicle started and every moving vehicle stopped. Freak occurences of this sort have no place in actuarial tables that dictate current price adjustments. Despite my protestations the dealer 'screened through the information for himself and imposed a massive government surcharge on us, which rather took the fun out of our first trip home in the Stromba.

With Mr Dobson's directions firmly etched on my wife's memory we slid off in search of nutrition. The directions took us spiralling up crags of Couth and down through shimmering fields of Palanxas, their tiny blue shoots just piercing through the crusty flood plains. Later they would sprout the dark green horns of flesh that are indispensible with sliced Clovis. We stopped outside a domed dwelling, constructed apparently from the fossilized rib bones of the long since extinct Megamega, a huge creature, as legend has it, that grew quicker than it could be eaten, whose growth was stimulated by being eaten, and had no objection to being eaten. The perfect foodstuff, one might think, but in the end each creature grew so huge it was unable to crawl to another to mate and finally each one collapsed in on itself under the immense force of gravity on its vast bulk, leaving cathedral-like skeletons. These sank into the fine Megamega guano of the flood plains where they had lived and were revealed again eons later when meandering rivers cut fresh courses.

Our hosts were a pair of Copuli, permanently joined at the waist, as are all Copuli, by a length of gristle that they coyly draped in pink fluffy material. After marriage separation of Copuli can only be occasioned by death, disease or divorce. This unerring attachment to one another, whilst it can be considered charming, normally leads Copuli to choose other occupations than, for instance, running a restaurant. My wife and I rather wished that Mr Dobson had apprised us of this fact, but always in search of new tastes and experiences, we followed our hosts to our appointed table. We perused the menu in the dim, flickery light of a Noxule gas lamp, which spluttered and popped, and gave off a peculiar smell. The odd light seemed to make the vaulted roof of cream ribs above us jostle as if they were still inside some great breathless beast. I observed that what purported to be the menu seemed to be a list of contractual obligations on the part of the customer to eat what was presented before him in its entirety or face a harsh financial penalty for leftovers. I looked at my wife. She looked at me and almost at the same instant we laughed.

'What a marvellous idea,' I said. 'What an amusing joke.' Old Mr Dobson had spotted we had a sense of humour. This was obviously a trick the locals played on unsuspecting visitors.

Noticing our mirth the Copuli shuffled awkwardly over with a sheet of paper for us to sign. It was a copy of the menu. They seemed genuinely surprised when we signed it, with mock seriousness. 'Anyway,' I said to my wife, 'what can they possibly give us from Provender that isn't delicious?' We were soon to learn. A deformed long-haired creature, I had no idea of what species, hopped up to our table on one leg and presented us with an opened bottle of Halmatrope with no information on the label whatsoever. When I asked if there was any choice he shrugged and left it for us. I poured it. Its colour was good. It was lively, rather mischievous, as the best Halmatrope are, and, by golly, did it have a nose on it! Expecting disappointment I tried it. It was superb. We consumed it before the arrival of our meal and the waiter, unbidden, brought us another bottle. Then came the meal: there were no starters or puddings, just one main course, an enormous haunch of Nullion. I had never seen such a well-grown Nullion before and it was as lean and succulent as you could ever wish.

It was almost midday the following day when we finally

finished the last morsel. With tears of exhaustion and gratitude in our eyes we thanked our hosts and settled the bill. I joked about the penalty clauses in their menu and the Copuli laughed heartily as they and their entire staff helped us out to our Stromba. To our horror we realized we could not fit, certainly not both of us, nor it transpired individually. 'That was a damn expensive meal,' I grumbled to my wife as we waited in the flickering gloom of the restaurant's recuperation room for a taxi to take us home and a driver to trade in our Stromba for a size 14.

FEBRUARY

I bustled about in the kitchen preparing a snack. Our provisions were getting low. A slice of this, a lump of that, I worked with imagination and relish until the barrow was nearly full. Then, just to finish it off, I swatted all the Hully flies buzzing round the light and placed them decoratively on top to add a little crunch and fizz. I wheeled it through to my wife and we sat eating in the dining room, watching the early mists dispel from the valley.

We decided that the worst of the winter was past and that we had better set some plans in motion. We would visit the local plumber and Henry the builder that very day, Stromba permitting. It was an unfortunate oversight that, whilst it was possible to purchase Strombas in a range of body sizes, they all had the same size power units and hover fins. The larger sizes were therefore ridiculously underpowered and awkward to handle. We had one of the larger sizes. It was also time to retrieve our beloved Pallions from the local Marinade Stockade. We had refused to part with them when we came to Provender in spite of all our friends' entreaties. 'We'll look after them,' they said. 'They'll only get eaten there.' But no, come with us they must. We made enquiries and discovered that, for a fee, an enterprising pair of Montalbans would marinade your pets for three months in their own patent substance, guaranteed to render even the most succulent flesh unpalatable. Their three months was up. We hoped it would be effective.

As we mopped up the last morsels from our plates we reflected on how refreshingly guilt-free the natural process of eating is on Provender. Not for them the agonies of doubt

25

that wracked Conima not so many years ago; the vegetable riots, the 'Ban the Sauce' puritan protesters. Somehow Provender missed out on the entire interstellar debate. While the Universe agonized, Provender just ate. When the whole debate was so effectively resolved by the development of the Cognotron the people of Provender just shrugged as if to say 'I told you so'.

I can still remember what I was eating when the news came through – vegetable stew – even I was shamed off meat at that point. The Cognotron, developed to separate the minute life emanations from all creatures into a few narrow but definable groupings, had initially been harnessed to a group of common foodstuffs and also to the Project Manager's two Pallions for controls. The results were astonishing but all repeat experiments by rival laboratories had reached the same conclusions. The principle emanations from the animals were on the lower register, falling in groupings such as 'I'm hot', 'I'm cold', but predominantly, 'I'm hungry'. The Pallions just registered 'Feed me' whenever they saw anybody, at which point their tendrils waggled energetically. But the plants had all the surprises, only they reached the upper registers, often with complex combinations such as 'I'm cold, but I don't blame you', or 'Eat me if you must, I forgive you'.

These early findings led to a dramatic swing in the other direction, creatures started eating meat again, some ate their Pallions with a certain malicious deliberation, but, in time, everyone seemed to settle back to accepting that everything has feelings of one kind or another – too bad – we've got to eat. The creatures of Provender just shrugged with bewilderment at all the good eating time we had wasted.

I opened the garage door and the Stromba eased itself out, chafing its offside fins on a stone outcrop, an annoying habit it persisted with, despite repeated adjustments. We set off. It was a glorious day, still a little cool, but not a foam in the sky. As we sped by, I thought I caught a glimpse of Mr Skeg's head looking out from an upstairs window, but I could not be sure. We descended the valley to the village, Bepommel. We would visit the plumber first, George, a Razmoth recommended by Mr Dobson. I had tried to 'screen him first but, like most of Provender's artisans, he regarded the device with suspicion and loathing. For every worthwhile job it brought him it brought ten disgusting, unprofitable, distasteful little jobs or complaints. Imagine being woken at two in the morning to unblock the cloaca of a family of Drisks, or summoned out after a swarm of Melbum had perforated someone's entire pipework! George would, I hope, regard our visit as worthwhile.

When we arrived outside his dwelling, a complex web of pipework over which a variety of skins were stretched, he was sitting on his front step, wire-brushing some kind of manifold. He greeted me with a broad flash of teeth and a rib-crushing embrace. He seemed to know all about me. His friend, Mr Dobson, had mentioned us, he said. I told him what we had in mind: a new heating system, a new ablution suite and, maybe, an overhaul of the drainage system, we had no idea how it worked. This seemed to fire him with enthusiasm.

'Oh, no,' he cried, clasping my arm in a vice-like grip with his vice-like gripper, 'you must not touch that.'

It seemed the previous owner of our house, many years earlier when he had first bought it, had flown in an Ordure Consultant from Sprool, for many centuries the leading planet for waste management. This Consultant had weighed his client, made copious notes on his diet, secured a stool sample and core samples from the back garden to a depth of two hundred metres. Two months later, by which time the matter was pressing, a two-hundred-page report arrived, including aerial photographs and a recommendation to use the Silax B biodisintegrator with various optional extras, such as an auto-rodding facility, variable ingestor controls to handle the by-products of unusual guests and a maxi-boost unit for short duration heavy-duty purposes, such as dinner parties.

'Good heavens,' I exclaimed, 'I had no idea such sophisticated technology lurked beneath our feet. It must have cost a fortune.'

'That was the trouble,' said George. 'By the time he had paid for the Consultant's report he could only afford to dig a big hole like the rest of us, and get in twelve Drools with shovels every autumn to clear it. Don't touch it, works perfectly.'

We arranged that he should visit us the following day and give us an estimate for our requirements and, nursing my aching ribs, we bade him goodbye. Next, Henry the builder, another who avoided the 'screen.

Henry lived in a structure of such uncompromising solidity that one really could not fathom out how it had ever been built, unless the services of some subplanetary clearance plant had been secured at crippling expense. One enormous rock – the size of two normal houses – had been balanced on top of two smaller rocks – each the size of a normal house – and the front and back filled in with normal Henry-style stonework and windows. Whenever I later pressed Henry on the manner of its construction he would shrug and tap the side of his nose and say, 'Trade secret.' I learned later from one of Henry's labourers that a cousin of Henry's had stolen an MXK from the Sprool Plant Services bay, sprinkled the countryside with megaliths for family and friends on easy terms, painted it purple and sold it on to their main competition, Starflick, with forged documentation.

I hammered on the door with the specially shaped door rock they had left for the purpose. I had almost given up when Henry's wife appeared. I enquired generally about Henry's health and whereabouts. She seemed evasive. When I said that I had a job for him, quite a large job, and that I did not require any money from him, I heard a noise from behind her. Henry miraculously appeared, sleeves rolled up his enormous arms and a smile from ear to ear. When I introduced ourselves Henry nodded and said he had heard all about us from Mr Dobson and he was happy to be of service

28

to us. We arranged for him to visit us the next day, after George had finished.

'Ah, yes, George,' he said, 'an old friend. We often work together. Co-operation on such jobs is of paramount importance.'

We agreed – our project seemed to be shaping up well, and we were feeling peckish. We asked Henry if he could recommend anywhere to eat.

'Ah, yes,' he said, 'for sure, just around the corner, just the place for you.'

We followed his directions. A gaudy and poorly drawn sign hung outside a rather small, unprepossessing house. The atmosphere inside was smoky but we received a cordial greeting from a little brown creature almost completely covered in feathers. It directed us to a table near an enormous oven which seemed to take up half the room. There were twelve tables and only one was empty when we took our seats. A mixture of creatures, mostly male I noted, sat at the other tables, dressed in grimy apparel which one took to be their work clothes. They took no notice of us as they chatted and laughed loudly amongst themselves. They all seemed to know one another. Each table had a great jug of what I presumed to be Halmatrope with chunks floating in it and from time to time the creatures topped up their glasses. Some of them would pause now and again to roll dried Fust leaves up tightly, set fire to them on a small plate and inhale until they blacked out and their friends caught them. One so likes to see traditional habits continue unchanged in these remote areas. It is all part of the charm of Provender.

The feathered creature approached us and handed us a menu. I had noticed that none of the other tables had been given one. Furthermore, it was in Coniman, our language. My wife and I looked at each other. It was very enterprising and thoughtful of the creature to provide this service but we had made our choice to live on Provender, Provender was our home, we wanted no privileges. We could communicate adequately in Drool, Spheraglese – the language of most of the artisans – and a smattering of Sprock – the language of the intellectual élite. None of the latter actually lived in the vicinity, but they frequently descended on the area in droves in August from their crystal eyries in the Provender capital of Palissandria. We felt, therefore, a trifle insulted at our Coniman menu with all the delicious, mysterious Provender names for dishes reduced to stark lists of ingredients and technique.

'Thank you so much,' I said to the creature in the best Spheraglese I could muster, 'but what are these good people eating? We will eat the same.'

I knew I had connected. There was a roar of approval from all the other customers. Two actually came over and shook our hands. The feathered creature smiled and bowed and said, 'How kind,' as it left for a back room. My wife glared at me.

'What's wrong?' I asked. 'It's what we want, isn't it? Good traditional fare, the way the locals like it?'

'Yes,' she hissed through clenched teeth, 'but we don't want to pay for their good traditional fare too.'

'Eh?' I blinked.

'You confused your nouns and your verb and one word was completely wrong. You offered to feed the whole room with whatever they wanted.'

'Ah,' I gulped.

The serving creature emerged from the back room with four Drools stripped down to their shorts. As two flung logs in the oven, the other two dragged in carcass after carcass of all manner of meats and hacked them into manageable lumps with weighty cleavers. When the fire had heated the metal plates to a blue heat, these lumps were flung on and they leapt and sizzled and bubbled, filling the room with smoke and a delicious vapour which you could almost cut with a knife and eat. Our fellow customers looked at us with wide-open, grinning, dripping mouths – how could we begrudge them their meal?

We finished our jug of Halmatrope with its sweet tender chunks. I popped the last bobbing chunk in my mouth, savoured it and chewed it until it melted down my throat. I leaned over to our nearest table and asked the fellow what it was. Was it Water Grudge, I ventured, a well-known delicacy?

He looked at his friends and guffawed, then he looked at me again and said, 'Nah, it's Bladderat,' in crude Spheraglese.

'Surely not!' I protested, aghast.

'Sure as oi'm sitting here. The place is crawling with 'em out the back. Had you fooled too, tastes just loike Water Grudge so why pay fancy prices, just because it's got a few bad habits?'

I nodded. Sometimes ignorance is bliss. We resolved never to enquire what anything was in future – if it tasted good that would suffice. It is possible that the Bladderat does not deserve the opprobrium heaped upon it. As is generally the case, it is the male of the species that lets the side down. In the mating season lone males challenge each other for the dominance of the docile herds of warm, responsive females. At this time of the year the males drink heavily, causing a normally unobtrusive bladder to distend and swell horribly. If one such male encounters another each will attempt to direct a high-pressure stream of urine up the other's nostrils to deprive them of air for sufficiently long to cause uncon-sciousness. The winner, generally the possessor of the fullest bladder and deadliest aim, then has the pick of the herd. The losers, when they recover, spend the rest of the year at the back of cafés, eating leftovers and practising their aim.

At last every table received steaming plates bulging with a mixture of meats and vegetables. We followed our new resol-ution, if it tasted good we would enquire no further, and it all tasted good. I had assumed that these creatures would have a reasonable meal and then go back about their business, but no, as soon as one plate was finished another was set in front of them and us too, of course. After several hours my wife

31

suggested that perhaps, out of common courtesy as we were apparently the hosts, they might think it rude to refuse a dish while we were still eating. So, in a vain attempt to contain the escalating final tally, we reluctantly indicated that the plate we were eating would be our last. It did the trick. When we finished so did they. Before they left, each one staggered up to shake my palm and thank me and kiss my wife's feeler. We rounded off our meal with an Algarglanon and then came the moment of truth, the bill. Of all the days to leave our Credit Ratings at home this was ill-chosen; we seldom carry much cash. In the end they would only let us leave if we left them the Stromba as security. Yet again we travelled home by taxi. The Pallions would have to wait.

The next day George turned up promptly. Today would be good practice for my Spheraglese, I told my wife. She said nothing. We showed George round the house and he made notes, pausing at times to 'tut' and shake his head. When he had finished we sat him down with a Halmatrope and pressed him for his opinion. He gripped the glass tightly with his gripper.

'Melbum everywhere,' he sighed. 'They haven't penetrated the pipework yet but it's pocked all over. All have to come out.'

'All of it?' I gasped. We knew the heating system would have to be installed from scratch but we had assumed that the simple reconnection of a new ablution suite was all that was required elsewhere, apart from the extension.

'For sure. Now is the time to do it. And your ablution suite, I can do you a lovely triple pan set in Molarite.'

'You mean reconstituted Molar?'

'Well, yes, but they look lovely and they only need resurfacing every two hundred tonnes.'

'But the shaping?'

'I think you will find that the styling allows for yourselves

32

and any species you are likely to entertain.'

'We do have a broad range of acquaintances,' I warned, 'but to tell you the truth, we cannot stand Molarite, but it might do for the guest bathroom in the gratification suite.'

'Ah,' he said, winking. 'I can supply a broad range of gratification appliances myself.'

'Really?' I was surprised. 'They are not plumbing items, surely?'

'Some of them are.' He winked again, or twitched involuntarily. I changed the subject as quickly as I could.

'Well, anyway, we have ordered all that from Conima, and also our personal ablution suite, individually tooled in genuine Molar.'

'Ooh, the real thing, eh? Expensive. And the import duty too.'

My wife and I looked at each other. We had not considered that. We began to imagine the interminable delays through customs as Drools examined everything in detail and asked embarrassing questions.

'And the heating?' I steeled myself for the worst.

'No problem.'

'Oh,' I beamed.

'Probably take most of the year.'

'Ah,' I blanched.

'Now. As far as the fuel goes, have you decided?'

'Well, there isn't much choice here, is there? On any other planet we would opt for Solar power every time, but with the Provender Solar surcharge, a vicious, punitive tax as far as I can see, I refuse to.'

'Ah, well, the Sun is our Sun, so it is only fair to surcharge outsiders for its use.'

'But it's pumping out power the whole time, whether or not we use it.'

'True, true. Anyway, it's nothing to do with me. We can either fit the sleek, clean, efficient, practically invisible Solar

33

roof unit and the tiny storage units, admittedly at great expense or we can supply and fit a Noxule gas tank, the size of a house with sound-proofed burner manifolds the size of a room and heat emitters the size of a wall in each room, at a reasonable price. If you take that option you will need the waste gas disposal units and a visit every week from the gas tanker. Another half mile down the valley and we could have plugged you into the mains, but never mind.'

'You mean they wouldn't run the pipework that short distance?'

'Pricey, very, very, pricey.'

'Hmm,' I frowned. 'We'll let you know.'

George finished his Halmatrope, shook my palm firmly, grinned and left. This gave us just enough time for a quick snack and for us to regain our composure.

Henry was a little late, almost an hour in fact, and did not seem to be aware of it. He was certainly not apologetic as he greeted us with a wave of his enormous arms. We offered him a Halmatrope and explained our ideas to him.

'Planning,' he said, sinking so deep into our chair we had to look down on him.

I told him how our enquiries at the Bepommel Office of Enterprise had assured us that our house lay outside the disincentive zone and the size of our proposed extension and our Species Rating was within the discrimination margin.

'You never know,' he said mysteriously.

'What do you mean?'

'Planning is a funny business. You never know, you can be half way up out of the ground, minding your own business, when an inspector turns up and slaps an "Alien Intrusion Order" on you.'

I was about to remonstrate hotly on how we expressly wanted our extension to blend in using vernacular materials and local craftsmen when he leaned forward and slapped a huge forearm on me.

'Don't worry,' he whispered conspiratorially out of the

corner of his mouth, 'I have a cousin in the Office. Won't cost much.'

We showed Henry round the house and I gave him my wife's sketches of our proposals. He made notes and 'tutted' and shook his head now and again. We sat him down once more with another Halmatrope.

'Well?' I asked tremulously.

'No problem.'

'Oh,' I beamed.

'Probably take most of the year.'

'Ah. And the stonework. Can you match it?'

'Might be a slight hitch there. You see, this is Late Couth from the top of the quarry in its early days. The colouring is rich, the stitchwork is fine and it takes a beautiful polish on the lintels and sills. You can even spot the odd darts and pleats if you look close. Now your new, freshly quarried Couth is right down from the Early Couth strata, when your Couths had a fuller figure and took less trouble on the seams. Most of the colours have faded if, in fact, they were ever up to much. But,' his great arm once again dropped on me, 'I think I can find some second-hand Couth that'll be just the job. Cousin of mine is demolishing an old cottage in the middle of Bepommel.'

'Oh, how sad. What's going up in its place?'

'They're whipping up a Coniman Takeaway in mock Mollusc.'

My wife and I shuddered. What a small place the Universe was becoming. We waved goodbye as Henry drove off, promising to commence work as soon as possible. I limped back indoors, rubbing my aching body.

That afternoon, when we had finished a light lunch, we drove off through Bepommel and beyond, through lightly forested slopes of fast-growing Trake. Every so often we passed great clearings where the felled Trake trunks were piled high, waiting to be used for firewood. The bark made a tasty beverage and the odorous resin could be used to trap insects for savoury snacks. At length my wife spotted the sign 'Pallion Marinade'. We had not seen our Pallions for three months, visits were discouraged as they interfered with the process. They had been left at the Cosmodrome when we first arrived on the planet, in a special pound, so we had only spoken to the proprietors on the 'screen, which normally never does anybody justice. We drove down the track and became aware of the smell first and then we heard a baying, gurgling howl. We rounded a bend in the track and saw before us tank after tank of soaking Pallion. We looked at each other in dismay. We parked and the two Montalbans crept up to us, grimy, covered in Pallion down and smelling awful. One spoke to me. I recognized her from the 'screen.

'We have your two naughty girls in the shampoo and dry suite. They'll be so pleased to see you,' she said.

'I should think they will,' I thought, 'if they've only seen you for the last three months.'

The other Montalban crept off. Why is it, I wondered, that Pallion stockades, breeding banks and holiday suites are always run by two or three Montalbans, never the whole set? She returned with our Pallions, Mink and Pixie. They both jumped up at us as if we had only seen them yesterday, but the smell was awful, in spite of the shampooing.

'The smell will fade,' the older Montalban reassured us, 'and you can bring them back for a boost in a couple of years. Nothing will touch them now. I can guarantee it.'

I could guarantee it too. It was with great reluctance that I forced myself to touch them. We ushered them into the back of the Stromba and, opening all the windows, we set off home.

We had promised Henry that we would clear the foliage from the end of the house where the extension was to be. If nothing else it would probably make a good meal. In the event it tasted delicious raw, so we ate as we cleared and, before we knew it, it was almost dark and we had cleared much more than was necessary.

'Never mind,' I said, sitting on a lump of stone that had been exposed, 'this can be a patio for guests, in fact we can eat out here ourselves when it's not too hot.' I looked down at the lump of stone I was sitting on. It had markings on it. 'It's a sundial,' I said. 'I wonder where the gnomon is.' We kicked around the low foliage at the base of the dial. It was enormous once one saw it clearly and perfectly round in a rough sort of way, with a smooth upper surface. My foot struck something sharp. I picked it up. 'The gnomon!' I cried. It was ornately cast in Obloscone. I remember, back in Conima, my grandmother had an Obloscone hat for important occasions. The metal was obtained from tiny traces absorbed by Palanxas plants. Being adept at absorbing trace elements, if a field of Palanxas was sown over a faintly Oblosconic bedrock, in time, the roots could be harvested and the Obloscone leached out in microscopic quantities. It is perhaps a sad reflection on early Conimunculi values that the best that could be done with this rare and precious substance was to make it into headwear for the astonishingly rich. It was not then known, of course, that Obloscone was plentiful and easily refined on Provender and casually used for exterior purposes where durability rather than strength was required. Nevertheless, when its additional aphrodisiac properties, through skin absorbtion, were discovered, every scrap vanished. We were lucky to make this find. I was about to set it back in its appointed groove on the dial when my wife observed that if we left it there some Drool would probably make off with it. She picked it up and held it. I, of course, had already been handling it. We looked at each other and with one mind returned to the house, accelerating rather rapidly as we approached, taking the gnomon with us. We would have one made of a more inert substance for garden use we decided later, quite exhausted.

It was a cool but clear morning, so I ventured to take the

Pallions out for their first walk up into the hills above our house. We walked carefully along the path through the nearby vibrating foliage, so beloved by the Halmatrope, which Mr Dobson told us was called Putrage. Mink and Pixie seemed quite perplexed as the plants nudged and jostled them all the way. I hoped the fresh air might reduce their smell a little. When we emerged beyond the Putrage I paused to look down on our house nestling below in a slight dip in the slope, with its lagoon stretching far in front of it and the smoke from the kitchen Gaga drifting aimlessly up into the cool, still air. One of Provender's moons was still faintly visible, its mottled orange and green surface paled by the misty early morning atmosphere. What a contrast it was to the brown lump which Conima's once golden moon had become after centuries of waste disposal. What a brilliant solution it must have seemed when the first bulk transporters, powerful enough to ferry out the planet's entire waste problem to the arid airless deserts of its moon were developed. For two centuries the surface was piled high with everything Conima no longer needed. The first inklings of repercussions occurred when a random laser measurement showed that the moon's orbit was beginning to decay because of the weight of unprocessed waste, unable to change in any way on the inhospitable surface. In five more years, the scientists warned, it would dump the whole lot back on top of Conima. I presume that at this very moment they are desperately transporting it all to some other unfortunate satellite.

As I strode on up the hill Mink and Pixie raced ahead, scattering every predator for miles as their smell permeated the air. I thought I saw just the top of Mr Skeg's head vanish behind a tree, but otherwise all was silent and at peace. This was just what we had come to Provender to find. I called to Mink and Pixie; they were out of earshot, savouring their freedom no doubt. I waited until I was well and truly hungry but still they had not returned. 'They'll find their way back,' I thought and strode back home.

MARCH

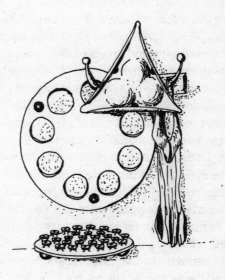

The early mornings were not so cool now and the mists dispersed quickly. I set off early to look for Mink and Pixie but there was no sign of them. Now and again a foam would pass but it always seemed to squeeze itself elsewhere.

There is a superstition on Provender that foams always squeeze on the Drisks. Enormous numbers of Drisks descended on Provender centuries back when their planet became contaminated as a result of an industrial accident. The giant Corto-Probax chemical combine set up a plant to process the huge desert expanses of Muriatic salts into the 'whitest whitener' as they described it. They miscalculated the instability of the tiny natural crystals and the excessive heat generated by the plant in full production. This vapourized a tiny amount of Smolene fat in the company canteen which proved to be the catalyst in triggering off a chain reaction across the planet. All the tiny Muriatic salt crystals absorbed the heated atmospheric water vapour and expanded into gigantic sesquiplicate crystals. The unstoppable reaction left the planetary surface uninhabitable and the atmosphere so dry that the Drisks' lungs withered and shrank. All the Drisks that could left in one of the most sudden and immense diaspora of recorded history, settling in groups in almost every habitable system. Their planet first became a giant glittering orb with innumerable facets and finally stabilized into a vast dodeca-hedron, considered to be one of the hundred wonders of the universe. As galacto-transporter after galacto-transporter of sightseers marvel at its beauty they tend to overlook the fact that it was the worst example of industrial pollution ever experienced.

The hapless Drisks do indeed seem to bring their own luck with them. I myself have seen foams fighting against the prevailing wind to squeeze themselves on the small community of Drisks to the east of Bepommel. I have no doubt that the final destination of the winter's freezing green vapours that froze us was to spiral for weeks on end around the Drisks. I had contacted Trevor, a Drisk, on the 'screen the night before. We needed someone to check the lagoon ready for the summer and he came highly recommended by Mr Dobson, even though he does not possess a lagoon himself. The 'screen flickered and went blank several times during our conversation, something which it never normally does, and I was reminded of the Drisks' general misfortune with technology. However, he was the only Lagoon Expert we knew about in the area. We realized that the Provender approach to work was different from our own and that it was we who must adjust and not them.

Trevor was rather later than expected. We had given up hope entirely and were in the middle of a cold collation when I heard the approach of an exceptionally loud vehicle. It was Trevor, driving one of the earliest Stromba I have ever seen. Never lavish with design, the earliest commercial Stromba looked like something you would fatten Trivets in and with their profanatory power unit they were loud and notoriously unreliable. In short, the last vehicle a Drisk should ever have considered purchasing. Trevor was apologetic. The Stromba had, he said, questioned his orders, deliberately misunderstood his directions and then returned to its garage and refused to come out. I sympathized, explaining how mine had developed the annoying habit of chafing itself on a rock every time it left the garage, and he obviously viewed me from then on as a fellow sufferer, an honorary Drisk.

He followed me to the patio pontoon, remarking on our floating chair.

'A Flasted 49 with adjustable trim and notchable

42

extremity supports,' he enthused, 'you don't see many of those.'

'We brought it with us in our allowable personal house effects.'

'Dodged the tax, eh?'

'Certainly not, we declared it and they classified it as a soft furnishing.'

'Probably never heard of a Flasted 49. I've only ever seen them on the covers of luxury catalogues. Does it have a lazarette?'

I lifted the hatch, he was impressed. He leaned forward to touch it but I prevented him and led him away to the filterhouse.

'Any problems?'

'Not yet, but I've heard that in a few weeks, when the Grebble mate, every upland lagoon is a mass of spawn. I've nothing against Grebble, they taste delicious, but . . .'

'You don't need to worry about them,' he reassured me. 'Every year there's a panic but I've never yet seen enough Grebble to challenge these units.' He smacked the filter pipework confidently and it started to make a whirring noise.

'What's that?' I asked. 'It's normally silent.'

'Just a little vibration I expect, soon pass.' He shut the door and we moved back to the pontoon. Drisks can stay immersed for long periods of time between breaths so they are ideal for lagoon maintenance.

'I'll give it a few more weeks to warm up then I'll come over and check her through from end to end.'

I thanked him. We knew from experience how soon a lagoon could turn from a pleasure into a liability. In Conima airborne contaminants were the main problem. A passing flock of Drilch, which only excrete over water and then by reflex, could ruin afternoons afloat with friends. Bacterial infestations could raise the temperature sufficiently to melt your floating chair, if left unchecked. Just in case Provender had its own problems we wanted our lagoon tested before our friends descended on us for the summer. There is nothing worse than a lagoon in close proximity to your house that has gone wrong on a hot day.

Trevor left, and I heard him disappear down the valley. Indeed, it was probably possible to hear him drive all the way home. Just as you thought he was out of earshot he would start to get louder again which was either his Stromba straining uphill or possibly mischieviously retracing its course for a mile or two just to annoy its owner.

My wife called me. Someone was on the 'screen from Conima. I rushed in but did not recognize the face.

'You don't know me,' he said, 'friend of a friend of Eric and Sybil.' I was still no wiser. 'Told me all about you. Sounds just the job. Fancy a piece myself. Weather here's atrocious. Be there tomorrow. Contact you then. Bye.'

The 'screen went blank. I don't think I had managed a single word. We had not spoken to Eric and Sybil for years, let alone told them of our whereabouts. I thought no more about him until two days later when I was awoken early by the 'screen. It was the friend of the friend of the friends.

'Morning. I'm here,' he warned.

'At the Cosmodrome?' I mumbled, still sleepy.

'No, at Bepommel. Had an appalling journey. This place is dead. Had to be most insistant to use this 'screen. None of them speak Coniman. Can you pick me up?'

'Where are you?'

'In the middle of the place by that disgusting public ablution pit. Filthiest thing I've ever seen.'

'Quite, quite.' I did not want to hear any more attacks on Provender's quaint devices so I arranged to pick him up as soon as I could. Before leaving I gulped down a strong black Robusta to wake me up. I opened the garage door and the Stromba went out of its way again to chafe against the rock as it emerged. I did not hurry to Bepommel, the impatience and short temper our Conimunculi guest brought with him were easily absorbed as I knew from the past. I would not allow myself to be affected. Instead, I savoured the strong bitter aftertaste of the Robusta – not many have the chance to grow as big as that one had been, not in our kitchen, anyway – and marvelled at the dazzling array of colours in the countryside.

I pulled into the side of the track. There, far, far above hovered a Woolly Throat Piercer, a rare and beautiful sight. These creatures never land. They are conceived and born in mid-air, eat, sleep and everything else in mid-air. Their droppings hover for weeks on end, often sticking together beneath the flocks forming enormous evil-smelling mats which suddenly drop for no reason, often on Drisks. My uninvited guest was waiting, irate and dishevelled near the ablution pit he found so offensive. Already, early-rising Bepommel residents who could not afford ablution suites of their own were slipping round behind the scant weather-worn graffiti strewn boarding.

'At last,' he spluttered. 'Thought you'd be here sooner. Whatever happened to the Ferenziculo?' He regarded my Stromba with ill-concealed disgust.

'Whatever happened to you?' I countered. His appearance was not in accordance with his manner.

'Had to use that filthy thing.' He nodded at the ablution pit, obviously unable to even bring himself to utter its name. 'Been a long journey. Never seen anything like it before, lost my footing. Some Drisks had to pull me out.' This last detail was evidently the worst part of it.

'That's fortunate,' I said.

'Hmm,' he grunted with no hint of gratitude. I drove us home.

My wife had stocked up in the market the day before and an enormous breakfast awaited us. The choice still reflected the limitations of the season. In a few more months the markets would be overflowing with Provender's delicious summer delicacies.

45

Our guest arrived at the table, washed and changed and evidently in better temper when he saw the food. He gulped it all down, scarcely pausing for breath, then, as we finished our meals with less haste, he amused himself by walking around the room, snapping up everything that moved. My wife and I looked at each other.

'Don't let him near the Robusta,' I whispered and she cleared away the plates and made sure the cupboard under the kitchen sink was firmly shut.

'I'm an Image Transmuter,' our guest confided as we showed him round the house. We had guessed as much. 'Remember that business with Pontius B?' We nodded. 'Shocking, shocking business, but who put it on the map? Just another boring outer planet until they secured our services. And then afterwards, who cottoned on to the business potential of franchising the idea? Opened up a whole new set of galaxies for development. Sent my Credit Rating off the register. So. That's why I'm here. Want a little place for the odd weekend. Not as little as this, you understand. But cosy. I've arranged to meet an agent this afternoon. Look around a few. Trouble is, they only speak Spheraglese, would you believe it? So I'll need your help.'

'Ah.' I fought for composure. 'If only I'd known. We have an appointment straight after lunch.' In fact, we had promised ourselves to have another good search for Mink and Pixie. We knew they would never starve on Provender but we wanted them back, and all the fresh air must have helped reduce their smell.

'Oh.' He seemed put out. 'If you're sure then. I'm sure I can make myself understood if necessary.'

'Oh, I'm sure they'll understand you completely,' I said, catching my wife's eye.

'Right. Mind if I use your 'screen?' I said no and we did not see him for the next hour. He emerged when he smelt a snack on the way.

'Oh, jolly good. I'm famished,' he said, and downed the

lot, including ours. My wife went off to prepare some more and he confided to me in hushed tones, 'Doing the big one at the moment.'

'Oh, what's that?' I asked.

'You know, this IDS business, Intellectual Deficiency Syndrome, they're all so scared about. Got to eliminate the myths, put it in context.'

IDS had been the main topic of conversation at every dinner party just before we left Conima. Threatening as it did only Conimunculi of higher intellect, it was chic to be considered at risk. Rumours abounded as to exactly how one could contract it. Some said a full and frank mutual exchange of ideas with an infected person, others claimed to have caught it from a laboratory seat, but the truth was, no-one was quite sure. In the meantime, it was incurable, reducing intelligent influential Conimunculi in their prime to little more than weavers, thatchers and upholsterers, common obsessions amongst the terminally sick. A close friend of ours was struck with awful suddenness. One day he was running a Halmatrope-importing warehouse, the next day his wife woke up to discover him folk dancing. Tragic.

'The big one,' our guest repeated, nodding ominously.

'You're quite safe then,' I thought.

When our guest had departed reluctantly, borrowing our Stromba, we set off in search of the Pallions. As we wound our way up through the Putrage I spotted Mr Dobson in the distance, bent double. We fought against the jostling foliage to reach him.

He looked up as we approached. Apparently he was pruning back the poorer shoots with low motility. He warned us that he was expecting a poor year this year and any reports we might have heard from neighbours that his crop yielded exceptional quantities of high quality Halmatrope year after year were exaggerated. We said we had heard no such thing and he seemed relieved. We said that we should not be disappointed; 'On the contrary any

47

bottles at all will be a bonus since we had not expected any at all when we bought the house.'

He seemed genuinely cheered and snipped away with renewed vigour. We asked him if he had seen our Pallions at all. He asked us if they smelt awful, we nodded. He had seen them heading towards Mr Skeg's house. We left him to his labours and decided that now was the time to introduce ourselves to the reclusive Mr Skeg. We followed a path back downhill, past our house, and on to Mr Skeg's cabin. It was surrounded by a high fence and it was some time before we discovered a section that opened. He obviously intended to deter uninvited visitors. We beat our way to the cabin door and tapped lightly. The whole cabin appeared to be constructed of Trake, a poor timber, generally deemed suitable only for firewood. Little attempt had been made to remove bark and branches. The trunks had been heaped together clumsily and yet it was not possible to see anything through the gaps and cracks, nor through the tiny, smoky windows. I spotted Pallion tracks in the soft ground outside. The door opened a little and an eye was just visible, twinkling.

We introduced ourselves. Mr Skeg opened the door wide and stood before us, short, stooped, but apparently all in one piece.

'Come in,' he croaked in Spheraglese with a peculiar accent. 'First guests of the year. I've regenerated earlier than usual this year. Food turned up on the doorstep yesterday, quite unexpected. Tasted foul, but you can't complain at my age, can you?'

We followed him in and marvelled at the interior. The Trake exterior was obviously a deliberate concealing device, for inside the walls were thin, polished slices of Late Couth and the ceilings were of heavily moulded plaster depicting the tastiest animals of Provender. Mr Skeg noticed our admiration.

'You don't see work like that any more,' he croaked. 'My grandfather had it done, got one of your real plasterers

48

over, a sixth generation artisan, genuine Ochran. Came to settle in the village. His family's still there.'

I looked closely at the detail. It had withstood the years well, with just a little staining from the open fire.

'Mind you, trouble to work with, Ochrans.'

'Oh?' I said, unfamiliar with the species.

'Temperamental, alternate sex from day to day. One day nice as pie, the next, argumentative, pugnacious . . .'

This seemed a timely warning as we were about to have the builders in, but if we could coax one ceiling like this one from a plasterer it would be worth a great deal of tolerance and persuasion. However, we had no idea what Henry's work force consisted of.

Mr Skeg offered us a drink. He prepared an infusion of Trake bark and left it to soak.

'I get my own bark,' he explained. 'You've got to select it all before the end of September, the thickest bits down near the ground. Then you hang it up to dry out and hope the Hully flies will take to it. If you've picked well they'll lay their eggs all over it.'

'Ah, I see, it's the eggs that give it the flavour,' I said.

'No, no. Then your Robusta eat the eggs, and they have an emetic effect. The Robusta disgorges its stomach contents on to the bark and the acids break down the cell walls.' He poured us all out a cup.

'So that's how you do it,' I said, swirling the hot, dark liquid around, with reservations about consuming it.

'That's just the beginning.' He settled back down in his chair and was evidently warming to the subject so, as he drew breath ready to continue, I swiftly broached the subject of Mink and Pixie.

'Two Pallions, you say?' he repeated after me. 'No, no, don't see many of them hereabouts.'

I was going to remark upon the footprints outside his door, but instead I said, 'We've just had them marinaded for their own sake, of course.'

'Oh,' he said and was pensive for a few moments. 'Does it do any harm, this marinading?

'Just makes them unpalatable, they seemed in fine health.'

'No, I mean if, er, anything eats them?'

'Oh, I don't think anything would be that desperate,' I laughed, and he nodded. But I did think, fleetingly, later, that you would also have to be pretty desperate to start eating yourself, as Colwigs are rumoured to do in the winter. Mr Skeg assured us that if he saw the Pallions we would be the first to know.

He sipped his infusion and we did likewise. My wife and I agreed later that it was not worth all the trouble Mr Skeg had been to to produce it, but we complimented him warmly on it at the time.

'Never had it before?' he grinned. We nodded. 'Acquired taste. You'll see. You'll want it again. You'll see. Be making your own one day. You'll see.' He was most insistent. We thanked him and set off back home, feeling slightly disorientated, but the feeling soon passed. When we reached our house we stopped and looked up at the hills beyond and imagined Mink and Pixie cavorting among all the exciting new scents and flavours.

'They'll be fine,' I told my wife. 'They'll turn up when they're ready. We shouldn't worry.'

I noticed that the garage door was shut. The Stromba was back and our guest was in the kitchen gorging himself. The cupboard door under the sink was ajar and he greeted us with a full mouth, which he emptied in one great gulp.

'There you are. Felt peckish. Helped myself. You don't mind?' We told him to make himself at home. He needed no encouragement. We sat down in the sitting room and he told us how his afternoon had gone.

'Fiasco. Showed me a grubby little shack, no lagoon, no ablution suite, Noxule gas tanks the size of a house, burner manifolds the size of a room, heat distributor the size of a wall. I snatched away their details and looked through until I saw that what I was after was on the cover of their lists. Then I pointed to it. They laughed. Fancy having a picture of the Parliament Building on the front of their details.'

'They are called "Parliament Properties",' I noted, seeing their details on the table.

'Anyway. Cut a long story short. Saw just the place. Made an offer. Getting it. Bit of a way from here though so I probably won't get down here much.'

'Never mind,' I consoled.

'So, I'll be off first thing. Be in touch though.'

'Oh, good,' I lied.

Early the next morning a taxi collected him for the Cosmodrome, just as Henry turned up to start work in a heavy duty transporter, loaded up with equipment. He parked by the spot we had cleared.

'Fine vehicle, Henry,' I remarked.

'These Julex never let you down. Hasn't let me down once, this one. They just go on and on.' Two helpers of similar build to Henry got out and were introduced as Alf and Don, cousins of Henry's. I went inside for breakfast and when we had finished a few hours later we found their vehicle empty and the three of them hard at work digging out the foundations. I remarked that they appeared to have made no measurements or markings and Henry took me to one side as his cousins laboured on.

'You want it to match, don't you?' I nodded. 'Well, I got to stick to the old methods, like my father and my father's father.'

Hoping my Spheraglese would see me through the coming months I endeavoured to explain that we had ordered various suites of specific sizes to be accommodated in new rooms of specific minimum sizes and he assured me that he understood. The surface of our land is covered by a thin layer of creature droppings and shed foliage. This was easy to dig through. Below lay a harder layer of long discarded bones and dwelling remnants mixed in with older compacted sediments like the top layer. This proved hard work, even for this muscular trio. Just before lunch they paused for a snack and within minutes all three were fast asleep in the sun. I took this opportunity to check the measurements of their trenches. They bore no relation to the plan. I tried to shake Henry awake, but he remained fast asleep all the rest of the day. I just caught him before they tried to slip away at twilight, thinking we were immersed in a meal. We were, but I was ready.

'First day,' he assured me, 'always the hardest.' Next day they would double-check and make any corrections.

Nobody turned up the next day, or the day after, and Henry's 'screen remained unconnected. I was prepared to pay a visit to Henry on the third day when he turned up with his cousins, apologizing profusely that his Julex had let him down, for the first time ever.

I remarked that it seemed in perfect running order now and he grinned and agreed. They spent all morning filling in the erroneous trenches of their previous effort with the spoil from the fresh attempt. My wife gave them each a Robusta and I checked the layout. It seemed to be accurate enough this time. It was certainly within the margin of error we had understood was only to be expected by Provender artisans. By the evening the trenches were finished. Henry and his cousins had vindicated themselves.

Sadly they did not turn up again for three days. When they finally arrived I asked Henry how his Julex was. He seemed surprised. 'Why, it's in perfect running order, no, the delay was the Moostrin.' I asked him why he had not anticipated the need for the Moostrin and ordered it earlier to guarantee its prompt delivery. He laughed and I had the idea that Henry's supplies of Moostrin, through, I believe, another cousin, were not ordered through the usual channels and might turn up at odd, unexpected times in inappropriate vehicles. Henry and his cousins sat in the shade all day waiting for the Moostrin. I offered to let him use the 'screen to chase it up but he said it would come in its own time.

My wife and I decided to go out for an evening meal and when we returned Henry and his cousins were just finishing smoothing off the Moostrin in the dark. We noticed enormous tracks all round the house picked out by the Stromba's lights, and that one of our gateposts was on its side in a ditch. Henry assured us that everything was going to plan and that the Moostrin would now require several weeks to cure before they proceeded further. My wife and I looked at each other in the light of our front doorway and back at Henry's broad, grinning, unflustered face. This was the way things were done on Provender. We shrugged and said we would see him when we saw him and they drove off into the night singing.

We stood outside for a little while, looking up at the sky and all those faraway worlds, wondering what lay beyond. Before we had left Conima the astronomers had sent an artificially intelligent telescope into space, powerful enough to look back at the beginning of the universe. The first time it was activated they glimpsed the sole of a massive foot, just vanishing from view. Then the image blurred. Tests revealed that the telescope had become short-sighted and a special pair of corrective glasses were flown up and fitted at great expense, but the telescope was too self-conscious to be seen in them. Eventually a set of contact lenses was formulated and fitted but whatever the astronomers had hoped to see was gone. Forced, perhaps, to retreat even further back in time from scientific probing.

APRIL

It was already warm, even though it was still early morning. I looked across the lagoon. It seemed to be set on fire by the sun rushing up from the horizon. There was not a foam to be seen and the upper atmosphere flashed and shimmered as the sun's rays heated it. When the more remarkable effects of the sunrise had begun to subside I noted that the surface of the lagoon was not as it should be. I raced downstairs and gulped down a Robusta. On close inspection the surface of the lagoon was solid with Grebble spawn and the overworked filterhouse was beginning to emit a thin plume of blue smoke from under the door. I rushed in and switched it off, then I called Trevor. He seemed unmoved and not at all repentant about the assurances he had given us.

'It's never as bad as it looks,' he soothed. 'I'll be straight over, soon have it fixed.'

Trevor reached us, loudly, just after lunch. We had capitalized on our windfall and had been eating Grebble spawn all morning in a variety of recipes; raw, grilled with a dab of Smolene, mashed on top of devilled Nullion and even finely diced together with something I caught in the corner of the filterhouse which was obviously in its prime. This was making no inroads on the problem, however. Trevor stood on the lagoon pontoon and scratched his heads. 'Well, I've never seen that before,' he said.

'What can we do?' we asked desperately. Taking advantage of Henry's absence while the Moostrin cured we had invited guests to stay. A plague of Grebble would not be their idea of a holiday, or ours.

'I'll spray it with an Instamort maxi-canister,' Trevor suggested.

'We don't want a lagoon full of dead Grebble any more than we want one full of live Grebble,' I snapped.

'Melek,' Trevor said. 'Voracious, insatiable, ten of those will clear the lagoon in no time.'

'And then we have a lethal lagoon?'

'No, they can be recaught simply with a baited trap. When the Grebble have all gone they'll soon get hungry again, then they throw themselves into the trap. All over.'

It seemed the only answer. Trevor noisily departed to purchase some Melek and we prepared for our guests. The first stop was the Bepommel market. It was still busy when we got there and we realized that this was the first really hot day of the year. Nevertheless, a small foam rushed in and squeezed over a Drisk stall selling small emulsified slabs of fermented Nullion skin secretions. Our mouths watered as we passed great green sheaths of Brotch hanging up to dry and pink and purple Matchugan and Hollombrost. On the meat stalls, small hairy Ansates hung by their handles in neat rows and Pataguins lay outstretched, surrounded by endless filleted slabs and flitches of meats we could not name and whose tastes we could scarcely begin to imagine. We loaded up the Stromba and I reversed up to the front of one of the Bepommel Halmatrope warehouses. I had been there several times before and knew the proprietor was a friendly Drool. I explained that we were expecting friends from Fractin, a most discerning planet. They would appreciate a fine Halmatrope almost as much as we did. The proprietor suggested a number of suitable choices, one of which, he pointed out, was being produced quite near Bepommel by a Mr Dobson. I affected only polite interest.

'Why, yes,' he elaborated, 'an exceptionally high quality Halmatrope, produced year after year in great quantities from such a modest-sized patch.'

I purchased three bottles, along with a dozen others, and

we set off home, the Stromba lurching awkwardly round the bends and straining up the hills.

When we got home we sat on the patio and opened a bottle of Mr Dobson's Halmatrope. It bore no relation to the pleasant but unremarkable bottles he had given us. Evidently one must expect this sort of dramatic variation on a small uncommercial holding. In the meantime we helped ourselves to Grebble spawn and filled every container we could find and put them in the ice room.

We expected our friends, Jan and Tony, to arrive just before our afternoon snack. My wife set about preparing something tasty and I cleared some of Henry's gear out of sight. The Moostrin had certainly set rock hard and it was all too evident that smoothing Moostrin in the dark was a bad idea. I was also a little surprised at the colour it was turning as it cured. All the household Moostrin I had previously seen was slightly mauve with bluey flecks. This Moostrin was black with a coarse texture, just like the new Bepommel multicraft bypass. I had also noticed, now that the curing was advanced, that it was starting to glow in the dark and when I spilt a little water on it the surface immediately roughened.

I heard Trevor approaching. He had a large tank in the back of his old Stromba. He reversed up to the lagoon, gingerly flung the top off the tank and the Melek, smelling the ripe Grebble spawn, leapt as one into the lagoon and started eating their way across it.

'There's hunger for you,' he grinned, as he pulled a clotted mat of Woolly Throat Piercer guano off his bonnet.

'Have you ever done this before?' I asked, realizing that I should have asked this earlier.

'This is your standard bio-degrader on Provender. Quick, clean. Well, I say clean. I mean, nature must take its course, with all that eating they are doing.' I was aghast.

'How can we clean all that out of the lagoon afterwards?' I asked. He looked sheepish.

'Well, Grebble spawn do a good job of cleaning lagoons.'

Jan and Tony duly arrived. They had hired a Stromba at the Cosmodrome and seemed amused by it.

'These hirecraft take a dreadful hammering,' Tony grinned. 'Takes the stress out of driving in foreign planets. I'd scream if I had to negotiate these trackways in the Plush-Planishade.' Tony was the proud owner of a vintage Plush-Planishade, once considered the most luxurious saloon in the galaxy. Fully absorbed in the interior, you can repose in the fourth dimensional fantasy of your choice, unaware that your vehicle is frantically reorganizing events around it to account for its problem-free movements. Nowadays, the possible repercussions of even the smallest trip in a Plush-Planishade are too daunting for all but the purest enthusiasts, so they generally disconnect the Positive Outcome circuitry and use the manual over-ride. It is then that the enthusiast, unclouded by four-dimensional fantasy and artificially induced safety matrix, realizes what a cumbersome old tub the Plush-Planishade really is. Give me a Ferenziculo every time.

Jan and Tony were most complimentary as they sipped Mr Dobson's Halmatrope and pecked at their snack. We had forgotten that Fractini do not possess our healthy appetites.

Tony is a Consultant in the Pan-Galactic law firm of Striffle, Striffle and Weave. It was his firm which negotiated the compensation after the Corto-Probax skin cleanser scandal, when the 'Miss Sentient Being of the Galaxy' competitors each received a complimentary promotional tub of the new formula cleanser. Never having tested the product to destruction under laser lights, the manufacturers were as dismayed as the competitors when, during the final line-up in lagoon wear, simmering under the laser glow, their skins peeled off and they all began to lift off the stage emitting an incandescent gas. Tony had overseen the complex pre-trial assembly of evidence, species tolerances and skin samples and still kept in touch with every one of his clients. To give the story a romantic twist, he had married one, Jan. Although not a Fractini by birth, he was able to have her remodelled to his taste with the generous compensation payments and thus was able to combine the stamina, intellect and deportment of an Ilph with the skin, secondary and tertiary sexual characteristics of a fully developed Fractini. They had been inseparable ever since.

We stayed indoors, in spite of the glorious weather, as there was rather conspicuous activity on the surface of the lagoon, where the Melek were thrashing around in an orgy of greed. We were also becoming aware of a slight smell as the waters changed colour. My wife brought in the Robusta and Tony broached the subject I had been avoiding.

'So, what about your Will then?'

'Yes, yes, I know,' I said.

'That Will you lodged with me from Conima is worthless here, you know. No use being squeamish. Take my advice, get it out of the way.'

'Later, please Tony, later,' I said. I was aware of a maze of restrictions in Provender law. You could not leave more than half your property to a Drool or Colwig, not more than a quarter to a Montalban and you could not leave anything at all to a Drisk. As I watched the lagoon froth and boil with activity I felt a calming pleasure in that pointed discrimination. We had encountered enough legal hold-ups in purchasing our property. I had 'screened Tony for advice on several occasions but all he could do was offer us the name of a Palissandrian law firm which proved to be extremely expensive. They would only correspond in Sprock while the vendors, who put the property up for sale immediately after inheriting it, refused to correspond in anything but Spheraglese. Then, to complicate matters further, the vendors, not closely related to their benefactor, fell out among themselves over what price to accept. It then transpired that two of them were half-Colwig, half-Montalban, and one had more than a touch of Drisk in him. This led to a protracted investigation by the Probate courts into who had a right to what. Our uninvited guest, the 'Image Transmuter', was probably in the throes of these problems at this very moment. That was comforting.

That evening we took our guests out for a meal. The Halmatrope warehouse proprietor had told me of a place that might interest our friends, and us. We took both Strombas and they followed us down through Bepommel and along the side of the old Crustal Vent, long since extinct. Under the shadow of the great Crustal Vent was the restaurant in one wing of an old, converted Noxule mill.

Centuries ago, when the vent was still active, the molten Drib hurling up from Provender's core, was channelled down through the mill, reheated using the Vent's waste Noxule gas, and cast for industrial use as the planet's most versatile metal. When the core puncture healed itself, as all minor surface blemishes on Provender do, the mill fell into disrepair and the Crustal Vent started its long process of disintegration. A local family of Drools, descended from the early millworkers, restored the mill and had a Noxule gas tank installed, hitched it up to one of the old Drib smelters and started a restaurant specializing in shell crimplets. The old Drib channels were flooded and stocked with live shell crimplets. Customers pick their own and they are boiled alive under the old smelters while you wait.

We made our selection then settled in the subdued lighting of the old converted batter house, where once Drools slaved away in cruel heat, battering the metal into submission. At one end of the room three Drools in traditional costumes stood singing traditional Drool 'Batter Songs' in their inimitable, peculiar way.

When the boiling tubs were ready we watched two cooks carry our live selection through, still thrashing their claws and snapping dangerously near the cooks' heads. It was all part of the showmanship. When they flung them in the scalding water their high-pitched screams temporarily drowned out the Drool singers. One of the cooks returned to reassure us.

'It's only the air escaping from them,' he said.

'That's all it is when I scream,' Tony observed.

When our shell crimplets were ready they were laid before us on Drib platters and we were each given an imitation batter tool to open them with. Tony and Jan were most impressed, they appreciated theme restaurants and managed to eat all their shell crimplets which was rather disappointing since I had been hoping to help them out. Tony bemoaned the inadequacy of Provender law on the question of food. On most other planets you could sue the restaurant proprietors if they failed to satisfy their customers, or inadvertently fed any species with food they were constitutionally unable to eat safely. This put quite an onus of responsibility on the proprietors of restaurants patronized by a broad range of species. The delicacy of one species could prove fatal to another. On Provender you ate at your own risk, and how we ate that night! Jan and Tony ordered course after course, we were delighted that their appetites had so improved. We finished with a Robusta and a particularly fine Algarglanon; I made a note of it for future reference. Jan and Tony followed us home. When we pulled up in the dark outside the first thing that struck us was the awful smell drifting off the lagoon. Whether it was that or the shell crimplets we shall never know, but something kept Jan up all night being very ill in the ablution suite. In the morning Tony did not look his usual dynamic self, either. We were very disappointed when they decided to cut short their stay, but perhaps it was for the best with the lagoon in the state it was. Two days later Henry turned up in the midday heat to look at the Moostrin, but took one look at the lagoon and left, which was most annoying.

That afternoon, with Trevor also incommunicado on the

'screen, we decided to pay a visit to Mr Dobson. He had been a most friendly helpful neighbour but so far had not invited us to see him and had always been too busy to accept our invitations. We would pop round with some of my wife's delicious Hully frickets, Hully flies lightly glazed in Smolene then roasted in the Gaga until they are so brittle they just melt in the mouth with a fizz. It was also a chance to get upwind of our sorry lagoon.

We had not seen Mr Dobson's house closely before. It was considerably bigger than I had expected. As we walked closer I realized that what we could see from our house was just the gable end and that it had a fine frontage and a range of outbuildings behind, surrounded by full grown Trake. Something growled from one of the buildings and Mr Dobson rushed out, saw us, then rushed across the yard, dragging all the huge doors shut before greeting us, quite out of breath. We chatted to him and he must have realized that we were not in any hurry so he eventually asked us to have a Halmatrope with him and his wife. We crossed over to the impressive house and past the great ornate front door to a small door round at the back. He led us down a long, dark corridor to his vast kitchen where we spotted his wife, a thickset rather ill-natured looking Drool. He introduced us and my wife presented her with the Hully frickets. Mrs Dobson just nodded and shoved them in a cupboard. Drools can only converse standing up so we felt obliged to remain standing out of courtesy, even though we were offered seats. The Halmatrope tasted similar to the ones Mr Dobson had given us before. Mr Dobson commented upon our lagoon but had no advice to offer. His wife, who had continued skinning some peculiar multilimbed creature, took an interest in the conversation when she heard we had Melek doing goodness knows what in our lagoon.

'Melek, fresh fattened on ripe Grebble spawn,' she remarked. 'Nothing to touch it.'

64

I said that I, for one, did not fancy touching a Melek from what I had seen of them. She grunted and returned to her skinning.

'Trevor will be selling them off to one of them Pallissandrian restaurants,' Mr Dobson said.

'Oh, no, he won't,' I said.

But we were too late. When we got back home we found a note from Trevor. He had trapped the Melek and taken them away. He would let the lagoon settle for a few days and then return. I walked out on the patio pontoon with a clear jug to see what state the water was in. No sooner had the jug touched the water than it was snapped from my grasp by an enormous Melek. My initial annoyance at Trevor's apparant inability to do one thing right was overshadowed by another consideration. 'Supper,' I thought, remembering Mrs Dobson's remarks.

I opened the garage door. The Stromba emerged, striking a small tree that I had previously considered safely out of reach. I drove it round to the lagoon pontoon, took the emergency tow-line from the back, tied one end to the Stromba breakdown hook – an essential fitting for every Stromba – and the other to a rock wrapped in a leaf. I figured the ravenous Melek would snap at anything. My wife came out to help. I sat ready in the Stromba and she threw in the rock. The instant the Melek snapped I shot backwards and dragged the Melek up on to the patio. It started to bite its way up the tow-rope to the Stromba as we emptied all our cans of Instamort on it to no avail. At that point I considered it highly likely that we would lose the Stromba so I got back in and prepared to accelerate away, hoping to shed the Melek. However, as I eased the brake, the Melek gave a great flip of its tails and we all shot forwards towards the lagoon. I pleaded, I begged, I cajoled with the Stromba. Just as the Melek was about to hit the water, taking me with it, the Stromba surged backwards and stopped. The Melek hit the bonnet with sufficient force to kill itself outright and badly dent the thin Drib metalwork. It was an expensive free meal I later remarked to my wife after the Stromba had been repaired, but we were both agreed that it was well worth the money for a gastronomic experience of a lifetime.

MAY

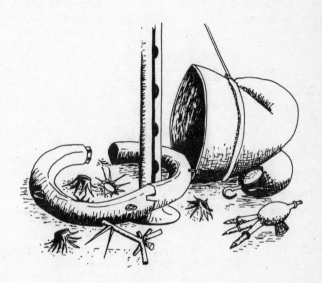

The weather was hot every day now. Almost as soon as the sun rose it was hot. In the middle of the day it was too hot to do anything in comfort outside. All we wanted to do was sink into our lagoon but Trevor had still not returned. Our skins were darkening and wrinkling wonderfully. We were looking and feeling marvellous. Any friends that 'screened us from Conima were envious the minute they spotted us. They all wanted to visit us. I wondered if our extension would be big enough. I also wondered if we would ever have an extension.

Henry seemed to sense just when our patience was strained to breaking point. We were rapidly approaching that state when he turned up early one morning with his two cousins. He flamboyantly inspected the Moostrin, tapping it with a small hammer and listening to the note it made, then he jumped up and down on it a few times and pronounced it fully cured and ready for the construction.

'A miracle cure,' I remarked, 'not merely ready for construction but also peak hour traffic.'

He eyed me warily for a split second. I smiled and then he laughed and then the cousins laughed too.

'All-purpose heavy duty Moostrin, all we could get at short notice. Last for ever.' Then he added, 'At no extra cost.' I had been vaguely thinking of reduced costs for the privilege of a floor that lit up the valley each night, but I realized that the logistics of bulk material deliveries in these country areas were probably a problem. After all, one of the attractions of Provender was that it was at least two centuries behind Conima in most respects. They had scarcely pronounced the Moostrin ready when I heard the rumble and vibration of an enormous machine. It was apparently another of Henry's cousins with the Late Couth from the demolished cottage in Bepommel.

Henry and his cousins worked tirelessly until midday, sorting, dragging and heaping the stones. We bought out iced Robusta and their remaining energy seemed to drain away, even as we spoke to them. Within minutes they were all asleep in the hot sun and resisted all attempts to awaken them until the early evening. This gave me plenty of time to inspect the morning's work. The stone matched beautifully and the ones that had been dragged into their permanent positions looked as if they had been put there when the house was first built. Progress was obviously slow but I was confident of the eventual outcome. Provender artisans are born, not taught. It was impossible to become a stonemason, a plumber or a plasterer if your father had not been one, and then his father would have had to have been one. Thus, even the mistakes were passed on from generation to generation. Styles changed little and every generation managed to find a few more short cuts and corners to cut. It was probably Henry's great-grandfather who first fell fast asleep most lunchtimes and now it was practically enshrined as part of their normal work practice.

While Henry and his crew slept loudly and obtrusively by their great stone heap, I received a visit from a Dribsmith I had spotted on a market in Bepommel. He had walked all the way bringing a gnomon he had fashioned out of Drib with decorative scrollwork for my sundial. He was short and thin for a Drool but bore the distinguishing marks of a Dribsmith: his batter arm was three times bigger than his other arms and his skin was speckled with scorch marks from the tiny pellets of molten Drib his battering sent flying. We slipped it on to the sundial. It fitted perfectly.

'It's fast,' he said, 'needs adjusting.'

I looked at the size and weight of the stone. It seemed

immovable. It must have always been fast. But apparently not. The Drool explained that Provender suffered from Incontinent Continental Drift. The three main land masses of Provender were formed on deep deposits of Smolene. This provided such effortless lubrication that from time to time, for no apparent reason, one or other of the continents would uncontrollably shift its position, sometimes sliding straight into another continent. Although this occurred over thousands of years and was seldom noticeable from day to day, it made the Provender sundial a remarkably inaccurate timepiece. I decided that it should remain fast.

Tired of waiting for Trevor to arrive, I had fished a few lumps of rotting Grebble spawn out of the filterhouse pump and nervously switched it back on. It did rattle a bit, which it never used to do, but there was no blue smoke. For the next few days I was forever fishing putrescent lumps out, but the lagoon was looking cleaner. It was practically back to normal when Trevor arrived one afternoon. He looked at the sleeping bodies of the builders and made some sarcastic comment, as if he were blameless, and inspected the lagoon.

'There you are,' he said, 'I told you it would be fine.' He then handed me his bill, which I thought to be a trifle excessive in the circumstances, and left, as loudly as he had come. The sudden cessation of sound not far along the road suggested that his old Stromba had probably come to rest for ever. He was wise enough to walk on home rather than seek help from us.

Day after day the weather was glorious and the extension was taking shape. Henry and his cousins were ready to fit the floor bearers. This variation from their stonework seemed beneficial for they managed to stay awake after their lunchbreak and remained fully awake all afternoon waiting for the materials to be delivered.

We had purchased a small quantity of suitably prepared Trake bark earlier in the week from a market stall. Mr Skeg

71

had been right. In spite of being unimpressed by it at the time, I had found myself slowly developing a strong desire to have some more. When I mentioned it in passing to my wife she said that she had too. After purchasing it, along with many other provisions, we rushed back home and prepared an infusion. Our first impressions had been mistaken, it was most certainly an acquired taste. We took out cups of Trake bark to Henry and his cousins as they waited for the delivery, and chatted to them. Alf and Don were brothers. They had both served on the Starflick refuse fleet before working for Henry, covering all the main pan-galactic communication lanes, vacuuming up stray asteroids and using them to balance moons with elliptic orbits.

'Some of these moons get to wobble so much they play havoc with your tides,' Alf explained. I had heard about Starflick's reputation. They won contracts by low-pricing, then instead of taking the waste out to the outer limits of the galaxy and firing it off towards the Great Attractor as all contracts stipulated, they would look for black holes to fly tip into, causing goodness knows what havoc in the other dimension. I asked Alf about this.

'Yeah, well, it goes on, you know,' he said. 'But I've never seen it happen.'

Don had been present at the clear-up after tests carried out using the Cyclotrex communicator, which, together with the Cognitron, is now of course banned in the Galaxy. Scientists experimenting with particle accelerators the size of a planetary system discovered that it was possible to actually communicate for brief snatches of time with scientists in the hitherto only postulated anti-matter universe carrying out identical experiments. Protracted snatches of discussion on a whole range of subjects led both parties to conclude that they had little to offer each other that they did not both already have, without cancelling it out, leaving nothing. The matter would have rested there if Starflick had not seen this as a perfect method for bulk waste disposal.

They persuaded the scientists to make arrangements with their anti-matter counterparts, who had a similar problem of waste disposal. They were to have an identical mass of waste ready. With perfect timing any amount of waste from one universe would cancel out a similar amount from its counterpart. This would solve for ever the waste problems of the two universes. However, the experiment misfired, the timing must have been out by a nanosecond, and the masses of waste from each universe passed each other midway and hit their opposing administration blocks with sufficient force to obliterate all maintenance records, blueprints and running instructions for the Cyclotrex. However, Starflick did not consider the experiment to be a failure. They continued attempting to operate the Cyclotrex, sending waste matter off, regardless of whether the outcome was mutually agreeable to the inhabitants of the parallel universe, or not. When this was discovered the use of the Cyclotrex was banned completely, leaving waste disposal as still the most intractable problem of the universe. Every year worse and worse waste bi-products are produced whose implications fewer and fewer creatures can grasp.

Since leaving Conima, we no longer receive the hourly state of the universe edited highlights, or the localized galactic updates. We suddenly realized that we were being drowned in information. It was not that our memories were beginning to vapourize, as can happen to middle-aged Conimunculi, but that there was too much information for any creature to usefully grasp. The properties of raw information have long since been known on Conima. It causes more information to form on its surface which, in turn, produces yet more. In the early days of discovery the planet Lumex, central newsgatherer for the galaxy, set about collecting and storing all the known information in the universe in high-density fractal codes. Millions of years ago that was a feasible task compared with now. As the experiment approached its goal all new research was stopped until

73

every last scrap of information was stored. This point was never reached. The exposed surface area of stored information, deprived of fresh superimposition, started to spontaneously speculate. In no time at all news broadcasts from Lumex consisted of pure speculation. How little things change. We do from time to time glance at the local news from Provender, mainly about food, and our friends keep us in touch with the plight of Conima, but we really do not have the time. Food on Provender is so time consuming.

Henry and his cousins gave up waiting for the floor bearers. Just after they had left the bearers turned up and the driver – some kind of Spansule – had to unload them himself with a great deal of grumbling. When he had finished I offered him a Halmatrope. This seemed to raise his spirits. He sat down on the pile of bearers and brushed his eyes back out of his hair. I could see he was not a native of Provender, he spoke Spheraglese with a slur. He told me he had lived on Provender for ten years, resigning from the pan-galactic patrol. I told him how much we loved Provender and he agreed, adding that not every creature took to the place. We were obviously fortunate to have found acceptance.

'You know what they say,' he chuckled. 'If they don't eat you in the first year, you'll survive.'

I laughed. I had not heard that one.

When he left, I noticed the delivery note stuck in the end of the pile of bearers. They were stained Trake and not the imported Strollon we had asked for. When he arrived the next day, Henry did not seem surprised at this mistake. He shrugged and said there was nothing wrong with good Provender Trake, and stained up who could tell the difference? I pointed out that he should know that Trake was a poor quality material and renowned for giving way without warning. We wanted something dependable under our gratification suite. He grinned affably and flung an enormous dendrite over me.

'Everything round here gets done in Trake, your traditional vernacular, renewable resource. Just think of the damage the Strollon loggers do, swooping down on a planet unawares, shaving it bare and then swooping off to the next one.'

I agreed that this was not a commendable practice but I had noted that all the floors and joinery in Henry's house were in Strollon. I made some enquiries on the 'screen. Strollon bearers had to be ordered well in advance. There was no chance of a prompt delivery. If we wanted any activity on the extension in the next four weeks we would have to settle for stained Trake.

Before he left that evening, Henry informed us that the bearers would need to be left to settle for a day before they could work off them to build the top storey. Coincidentally, as posters all over Bepommel had been proclaiming for weeks, the next day the fair was coming to Bepommel.

Even after the sun had set, the air was still and warm. We sat on the patio pontoon sipping a Halmatrope. Soon we would try the lagoon. I heard the shrill whistle of the 'screen, and rushed in. It was our uninvited guest, the Image Transmuter.

'Be pleased to know I've bought the place now,' he said. 'All mine. Shan't be down to move in for a while, too busy. Got a Drisk to keep an eye on it. Gave her your name. Must rush.' Then he faded from the 'screen before I could ask what he expected me to do. The first thing I would have advised was to keep the Drisk as far away as possible.

Provender fairs are renowned pan-galactically. The safety laws and punitive Species Rating surcharges on more advanced planets preclude all but the tamest sideshows. As we approached Bepommel we could hear the fair in action.

It was set away from the town on a flattened area of rough land where a Palissandrian construction company was hoping to buy permission for a processing unit for Advanced Palissandrians, as they called their geriatrics. This particular company specialized in warden-assisted blocks housing enormous numbers, their individual units were compact and yet lavish with luxurious detail. On every floor, serving every ten rooms, were communal areas stocked with a wide range of delicacies that were painlessly fatal. As soon as the inmate decided it had lived long enough, all it had to do was slither down the corridor and eat its last meal. These blocks were springing up everywhere, but the permission was too expensive so far in Bepommel and each year, as the company haggled over the price, the fair would descend and fill the plot with its dangerous machines, extortionate sideshows and unsettling, low-frequency music that rattled and clattered every loose object in Bepommel.

We parked the Stromba far away from the fair and walked to it. The noise got louder and louder as we approached, the vibrations juddered our eyeballs and the excitement mounted. We arrived just in time to see the hastily assembled giant whirly wheel, complete with seats full of screaming creatures, come unbolted and fly through the air, landing on the Bumper Stromba Rink, run almost entirely by Drisks with Smolened-back hair. We kept to the outer edge of the activities as machinery crashed and buckled, adding to the mounting excitement. Drools clamoured to ride in the Arm of Hunger which whisked them round and round until they completely evacuated their systems. Colwigs clamoured to ride the Wall of Fear until they were so terrified that relatives had to help them home with bags over their heads. Montalbans just clamoured. There was one dangerous ride left in action but even as we watched, all the springs flew out of the base and the counterweight spun off, out of control, and landed somewhere out of sight. As the Drisks dismantled the wreckage and packed it away for the next venue, every creature moved to the sideshows.

Scarred crossbreds in barrels glowered at each other as they histrionically tried to eat each other. Dribsmith Drools arm-wrestled with their batter arms for Halmatrope. Small groups of Montalbans cruised around jeering at other small groups of Montalbans. It was a riot of colour, activity and injury in the normally peaceful town. We were about to leave when we spotted Henry and his cousins trying their hand at the 'Lift the Megalith' stall. Alf lifted one end of the lintel clear of the ground; Don strained but could not budge it, then Henry, seizing it in his mighty arms, slowly lifted it and, raising it above his head, managed to place it squarely on the stone uprights, winning himself a Grebble in a bag of water as the cousins cheered.

With the sounds rattling in our ears, and the smells filling our heads, we stumbled back along the roads to our Stromba, remarking to each other how the excitement of a fair never seems to diminish, even as you grow older, highlighted by the larger-than-life, picaresque characters who are always associated with them. When we reached our Stromba we found it perched on two blocks of Couth with its hover fins missing.

It was with some difficulty that we managed to find a taxi in the busy town that evening.

Henry and his cousins returned to the stonework setting the stones on the upper storey. Work was slower as they now had further to lift the materials. As they slept through the hot afternoons we would slip into our cooling lagoon. The earlier trials and tribulations seemed to have left it unscathed, although the bottom was rather too slippery and the image of the ravenous Melek would now and again unnerve us if we bumped against each other unexpectedly.

One afternoon, as we restfully scudded across the pool on our Flasted 49, our skins wrinkling and ever darkening in the hot sun, our peace was suddenly shattered as one after another monstrous craft shot through the sky above us. We had forgotten. It was the annual Provender 'Round the Planet' Race. Entrants came from all over the galaxy. Most other systems have too tightly scheduled atmospheric space to provide a race window. We watched them roar by with bloated fuel tanks and unbaffled exhausts and we could feel the heat from them. In this conspicuous display of extravagant consumption the winner would not necessarily be the first over the line but the one who had consumed the most fuel in the fastest time during the orbit. Contestants were not permitted to refuel during the race. If they ran out of fuel and dropped from the sky they would be disqualified. Therefore, these deliberately inefficient craft, wasting energy in heat and sound and atrocious aerodynamics, had nevertheless to ensure that they had enough fuel to complete the orbit. Stringent regulations and pre-race inspections precluded the dumping of unused fuel except in emergencies. The event was sponsored this year by the Corto-Probax combine, one of the leading fuel producers.

The noise was sufficient to wake Henry and his cousins, something we had never been able to do. We headed for the patio pontoon and tied up. Craft roared by overhead at irregular intervals. We made some Trake bark infusion for all of us, hoping that now he was awake Henry would return to work, but they stayed put, watching the craft race by for the next few hours.

'Peregrine Bates won the last two years,' Alf said, 'son of Starflick's Managing Director.'

'Just another form of waste disposal,' I said.

'Life is just another form of waste disposal,' my wife added. We all looked at her.

The last few stragglers roared over.

'They'll never make it,' Don said as one stopped suddenly as it was heading for the horizon. A tiny eject module flew out before the stricken craft plummeted down into the distant forest.

Henry and his cousins struggled to seat one lintel and then went home. The extension was looking good. There was no fear of an Alien Intrusion Order here.

JUNE

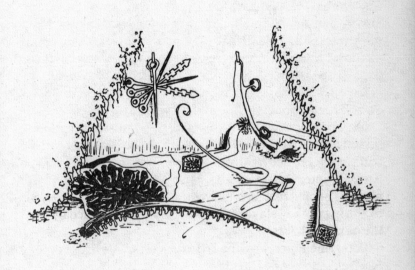

The weather was getting hotter. We made full use of our lagoon, but day after day after day there was no sign of Henry or his cousins. In our first optimistic schedules for the extension we had fully expected it to be completed by now and had invited a host of guests to stay all through the summer. We did not want to turn away any of them, but we were a trifle annoyed that we could not yet offer them the accommodation we had planned. I called to see Henry, the 'screen being blank as usual, and I saw Henry's wife. She told me that he had been called away unexpectedly and reluctantly to an emergency job at Felstine.

'They have a Halmatrope festival for the whole month of June there, don't they?' I asked suspiciously.

'Is that so?' she said with convincing surprise and ill-concealed annoyance. Before I could ask her to ask him to give the utmost priority to finishing our job she had shut the door.

Our guests were due to arrive from Palissandria in the early evening. We knew that they would be tired and they were never very hungry so we made sure that most of our eating was completed before they came.

Constance and Deverell had a multiplex at the very top of the Crystal Tower Building, the tallest artificial structure on Provender. On a clear day, they could see almost half of the planet's surface. An enormous power system, propelling the top of the building in the direction of the planetary spin, enabled it to keep up with the base instead of snapping off, as it frequently threatened to do when the power unit malfunctioned. It took courage to place one's trust in

Provender technology. I was envious of Deverell when they arrived in their Ferenziculo and I told him so. His Species Rating and government contracts had made its importation a quicker and less expensive proposition than it would have been for us, and the problems of servicing and fuel provision were dealt with by his company, style importers for the Palissandrian élite. They were both immaculately turned out as they abandoned the coolness of their vehicle's interior for the hot dusty air. They coughed a little as they picked their way over our uneven drive into the house and Constance stumbled in her needle heels. They were evidently as disappointed as we were that the work had not been completed. Constance was halfway across the sitting room when her needle heels became so deeply embedded in the old Trake flooring that we had to lever her up and carry her to a chair. They seemed intimidated by the Hully flies that flew in through our open windows and raced round the lights. They said little as they pecked away at the delicious Nullion my wife had prepared and retired to bed early, both complaining of headaches.

My wife and I were disappointed. We had brushed up on our Sprock so as to be able to make the most of the sparkling, intelligent conversations our friends always had with us whenever we stayed with them.

The next day was hot. Our friends got up early, obviously refreshed. They ate thin slices of toast rubbed with the flesh of Sprillet and the blackest Robustas we could find as we embarked upon our usual breakfast. In spite of the heat, they refused to go in the lagoon but seemed happy to watch us and chat as we paddled to and fro.

Deverell told us that business was booming and the wealthy of Palissandria were ever eager to seek out the best the galaxy had to offer, competing against each other for their positions on the pinnacle of taste. Constance and Deverell of course considered that they literally occupied this position in their astonishing home. They talked of humming wall coverings, hovering floor coverings and sympathetic decorations that adjusted to your mood. They talked of furniture that bonded with you, soothing and caressing away your stress. The latest line of fashions, they said, could be programmed to adopt whatever shape you desired to be, pulling you in in places, padding you out in others, or perhaps creating spellbinding effects at parties such as rhythmically undulating or completely enveloping you whenever you saw someone you wished to avoid. We felt left out of all this splendour as we sat in our light casual clothing, our deeply crevassed, dark skins radiating health. We had made our choice, to leave the hectic life of Conima that Palissandria tried to emulate, and enjoy the outdoor simplicity that all the rest of Provender had to offer.

'But what do you do all day?' Deverell asked us just before our snack. We explained that, what with learning all the languages, customs and discovering all the myriad things there are to be discovered on a new planet, we never had a moment spare. Of course, there was all the cooking to be done too and all the purchasing of supplies, our lives were fuller and richer than ever before: we were growing.

'Yes,' Constance said, 'so you are.'

We had hoped to walk up the hill with Constance and Deverell in the afternoon. We wanted to show them the views and let them experience the pleasure of walking among wild things that Palissandrians are never able to experience, but, being accustomed to personally adjusted environmental systems, they were feeling the heat and pre-ferred to stay inside the shaded but still warm house. We had a quick dip in the lagoon. When we came back they were asleep.

We had promised to take them out for a meal that evening and show them some of the life of Bepommel. When they woke up, they did not seem to have benefited much from their sleep and Constance's complexion appeared a little blotchy. We gave them some Trake bark infusion. They had never had any before and were polite but not over-enthusiastic. It seemed to do the trick though: Constance's complexion coloured and her eyes seemed to sparkle a little. They took us into Bepommel in their Ferenziculo. I sank back into it and. it held me firmly yet tenderly, as only a Ferenziculo can, with just that hint that only you and no-one else receives such special treatment. We went to the old Drib mill again. Constance and Deverell were a little dismayed at the singing Drools but we knew they loved shell crimplets. When they saw how large they were, they decided to share one.

The cooks carried out their carefully choreographed display, marching past with snapping shell crimplets held aloft and throwing them to their noisy death in the scalding water. Constance and Deverell were unperturbed by the screams. They were accustomed to the 'Fresh Houses' of Palissandria where gastronomes ate creatures alive, believing that any form of preparation, including a painless death, compromised the pure flavours unacceptably. The meals arrived and Constance found it difficult to wield the batterer but I assisted her. My wife and I had several more courses while they rested at intervals and worked their way through the first. When they had finished it they said that it had been exquisite but they were quite full.

As we relaxed with our Algarglanon, Deverell brought up the old Palissandrian dinner party debate – was Provender alive? We had heard similar debates on Conima, although there was never any doubt there that, were it possible for a planet to be alive, Conima was most certainly dead, and had been dead for quite some time. Various planets in our galaxy are credited with being alive by groups of scientists. Provender is one of them. The signs of life are deemed to be scarcely detectable on a daily basis, but are discernable by studying past records. The apparently random behaviour of the Incontinent Continental Drift seemed to be linked to any attempts at remapping the planet's surface. It takes many years to get anything to happen on Provender and on four previous occasions, just as soon as the complex procedure of precisely measuring and mapping the planet's surface was completed and the maps published, the continents would start their drift again and clusters of crustal vents would appear, disrupting the topography. A team of Drisks had also monitored the behaviour of foam. There had been talk of attempting to sue the planet for discrimination if it could be proved to be alive, but all their experiments had been washed away and the team leader drowned in a spectacular foam burst. We liked to think that perhaps there was a glimmer of intelligence and personality in the planet, and that it accepted us as warmly as we accepted it. Constance and Deverell refused to believe such nonsense. I could have cited the constant problems aflicting their Crystal Tower as classic evidence of a planet trying, as best it could, to rid itself of a tiresome thorn whose foundations pierced deep into its crust, but I did not. I could understand that they might be dismayed by such a thought. We decided to return home. The meal had been a great success. Constance was positively glowing when we reached home, and Deverell started singing, which was most unusual.

My wife and I slept soundly, as usual, and I was surprised to find in the morning that Constance and Deverell were slumped together in the ablution suite. They had not slept a wink they said. They had both been very ill. In spite of our entreaties, they got changed and we helped them down to the Ferenziculo. I reprogrammed it for the return route as Deverell seemed too groggy. They apologized for cutting short their holiday but they wanted their personal physician to scan them as soon as possible. We understood and felt so sorry for them. It was such bad luck, probably a bug they had brought with them from Palissandria. We felt grateful that we had such robust health and cast-Drib constitutions.

*   *   *

That evening, as we tacked back to the patio pontoon in our Flasted 49, we talked about Mink and Pixie. We had walked in the hills calling for them many times but still there was no sign of them. It was the one thing that marred our enjoyment of Provender.

We were accordingly overjoyed one morning to find a Riticule nesting on the sundial. The Riticule, a small winged creature covered in pink fluff, is possibly an archetype for the development of a whole new set of evolutionary criteria. Originally mutant, a Riticule must have been born which flew so slowly anything could catch it but, as it looked so appealing with its wide blue eyes and pink fluffy coat, nothing had the heart to eat it. More aggressive creatures probably flicked it aside with disgust. It had no idea of danger and therefore no thoughts of nesting in safe places. The early Riticule probably nested in foolish places, such as in the hover fin of a Stromba. When the owner found his Stromba would not start he would inspect underneath, see the adorable little creature and vow not to touch his Stromba until after the breeding season. Successive generations of Riticule nested in increasingly foolish places, halting transplanetary links by nesting on the heavy plant, disrupting Parliament by nesting on the Premier's podium and in a whole range of awkward locations for the rest of the creatures of Provender, most of whom resisted eating it. Ours had chosen our sundial which was fortunate. He was obviously not breaking new ground for his species. Had he been a Grade A Riticule he would have nested somewhere like on our Gaga and no amount of pink fluff or deep appealing eyes would have saved him there.

The Riticule is fortunately an isolated species on Provender, but it brought to mind the fate of other planets where excessive conservation zeal had more serious consequences. One remembers Guspage, a tiny little planet, crammed full of delightful species, each valued and treasured by the ruling Zealfin. When their advanced tracking system spotted the approach of a giant asteroid and predicted imminent collision, the powerful conservation on lobby, noting that a rare creature, scarcely visible to the naked eye, was breeding on the Asteroid Deflector launch pad, forbade the use of the pad until the creature's breeding season was over. This was unfortunately two days after the asteroid was due to hit. The matter was still before the committee when Guspage was smashed to oblivion. Then there was Illminon. Four hundred millennia of mistaken selective breeding totally upset the planet's evolutionary balance and a small family of dinosaurs became the first totally outmoded species to return to power. I believe there has recently been a takeover by a small faction of Trilobites.

With our guests making an unexpectedly early departure and our builders still immersed in some emergency job, we decided to pay a neighbourly visit to the Montalbans and introduce ourselves. They lived further down the valley beyond Mr Skeg.

We had breakfast and then later a snack. We did not want to turn up embarrassingly at a meal time and invite ourselves. Nor did we wish to go hungry. As we strode down the hill, tiny vortices of hot air zigzagged around us, whirling dust at our feet. When we could see the Montalbans' house, with its corrugated Drib roof and Couth walls of the same style as ours, we heard a shrill scream and one Montalban flew out of an upstairs window and landed rather heavily on an unsightly heap of Nullion bones. We stopped. The Montalban got up and limped back in the house through the open door. We heard it make an unintelligible statement in some kind of childish Spheraglese patois. There were several giggly sorts of noises from various of the inhabitants then a door slammed and we heard loud purring noises through the open upstairs window. They were obviously unaware of our presence. We decided to postpone our visit.

We had heard that the Life Force Donor Unit would be visiting Bepommel and we knew we would have to do our duty. Conimunculi have a very powerful emission, indeed it apparently has to be diluted for use on most other species. In the early days of Auraesthenics only crude measurements were possible and overdoses of Life Force to ailing patients were frequent and disastrous if unchecked, since Acute Charisma resulted. In those days an escaped Charismatic with access to multi-media could captivate a nation in next to no time, converting whole races to follow his or her pet foibles. Worse still, if these escaped before treatment was modified, and chanced to land on an unexplored planet, they could interbreed and change the whole course of the planet's history.

There is a well-documented record of Strepsle 3, a blue planet in a distant system with a few splashes of green. A Medicapsule of heavily sedated Charismatics bound for Misp 14 had crashed on Strepsle 3. They had all been passengers on a galacto-cruiser which was involved in a pile-up in dense nebula and had been inadvertently overdosed with Life Force to revive them. The Medicapsule had been taking them to Misp 14 for treatment of their Acute Charisma. The second accident left them unharmed but loose on the surface of Strepsle 3 for three days. Before the sedation wore off they had interbred with the dominant race who were rather undemonstrative materialistically but had a deep intuitive grasp of philosophy. In a few millennia the offspring had driven out their forebears and taken control. Now the planet periodically broadcasts pompous little messages in simple codes describing its inhabitants and asking if there is anyone out there? The rest of the time the galaxy has to put up with such a barrage of broadcast trivia that it pointedly ignores the place, except for a few joyriders in stolen Elipticons swooping over its surface, sometimes leaving graffiti in the fields.

We drove into Bepommel and found the Donor Unit set up near the market place. We sat in the queue and were duly placed under the phosphorescent grid. We seemed to lie there for no time at all before the nurse said she had had enough of us. On the way out we were given a Halmatrope, which made a pleasant change from the Conima units where you lie for half a day for nothing and then have a few hours of self-doubt to put up with before you revive.

JULY

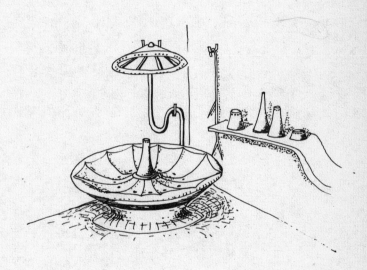

Henry and his cousins turned up unannounced. They looked tired. The job in Felstine had been demanding they said, a real headache. They promised that the Couthwork would be finished within a week and then a second cousin, Neville, a Traker, would come in and frame up the roof.

A friend of mine from Conima 'screened me to say that he was renting an ancient fortified Colwig winter house a few hours away near the coast, at the historic coastal town of Frenmahell. We had never been to Frenmahell before. The whole town was still largely unspoilt, built centuries earlier when local tribes of warring Colwigs would eat each other in the winter instead of themselves.

We had become so immersed in our new-found paradise that we had not travelled much further than Bepommel since we had been in Provender. After an hour in the discomfort of the Stromba we became aware of two things: one, that we had been wise not to venture far in our Stromba before and two, that to venture much further than Bepommel in any terrain-based vehicle was unwise in the summer.

Everywhere was packed with visiting species, all unable to converse with each other should their vehicles engage. We were stuck behind a heavy family of Dorf from the industrial planet of Manufex. Their hired Stromba was entirely unsuited to their body densities and the hover fins would spark against the hot black Moostrin on every bump. The two-hour trip had already taken us three hours. Every other species around us seemed to be Dorf. We were horrified. Their Credit Rating was currently so high that a holiday on Provender cost scarcely anything at all and with the Dorf's appetite eclipsing even Conimunculi's we feared the Dorf tourist invasion would literally deplete the planet. They were all heading to the sea at Frenmahell. Only the high, specific gravity of the sea in Provender could support the weight of a Dorf. In a normal lagoon such as ours they would sink to the bottom immediately and drown. It was a pleasing thought as we dawdled along.

I spotted the distinctive roof of our friend's rented house on the outskirts of the town. The owner had had the original ornate spikework restored at great cost and it glittered in the hot sun with a Riticule nesting on the topmost spike. The old fortifications were so effective that we drove round and round the house three times, unable to see any entrance, before our friend spotted us from an upstairs aperture and released the old counterbalance which tilted back a wall section for us to enter. It always annoys us how, in these days of comfort and efficiency, creatures are drawn inexorably back to the discomfort and inefficiency of the past. We feel it too.

The dank, musty interior of the house was fascinating. Maurice, our host, took us straight to see the Dolbury Joint in the great hall ceiling. This Joint, apparently, is known to Architectural Historians the whole galaxy over and has been replicated many times. It was first noted by Linus Dolbury who was inspecting the ceiling for a research project. The main joists had bare-faced soffit tenons with diminished haunches and two-face pegs. This was precisely the perfect joint favoured by the earlier Basilica builders of Strewth, but how had they evolved this joint and how had the technique travelled so far? We will never know. The soothsayers of Strewth foresaw a great famine. Their God was displeased, they said. They urged the builders of Strewth to construct a great Basilica, the greatest in the galaxy, and make an offering, the greatest offering any planet had ever made, to placate their God's displeasure. The builders of Strewth used every possible material resource on the planet to construct the massive, flashing cruciform Basilica, visible far out in space. This left the planet's population unhoused and also unclothed by the time the soft-furnishings were finished. Then they collected up all the food and drink on the planet and put it in the Basilica as the greatest offering ever made. This, unfortunately, led to the great famine which the soothsayers had foreseen and the secret of the Dolbury Joint perished with them.

Maurice had prepared us a special Conima meal. It seemed odd that he should have undergone the difficult and un-comfortable journey to Provender, famed for its own unique delicacies, only to cook us a Conima Casserole. In fact, we did enjoy the meal, and it brought back many memories of Conima, but we concluded on the way back home that one meal of Conima cookery every six months was quite enough. The recycled fibre and industrially manufactured nutritional additives are no match for natural food. It has been many years since anything could be grown on Conima. There simply is not the space. Even the old intensive methods in high pressure canisters proved too space-consuming as the population grew. We asked Maurice how he could bring him-self to return to Conima after seeing Provender but he said he was homesick. The word seemed to have a whole new range of nuances when he said it. He had brought all his food with him in shrink-sealed containers, practically weightless until water and air were added. His rented accommodation seemed to be deliberately chosen to keep off any encroachment of the real Provender, something which he seemed to hate and fear. I asked him why he had chosen this for his holiday destination and he said, 'To prove to myself that I could.' When we left, the wall swung noise-lessly back into place, sealing Maurice safely back in his lair, until the taxi came to collect him at the end of his holiday.

We braved the journey back home, feeling ourselves relax as we neared Bepommel and our beloved valley in the fading light. When we arrived home, Henry and his cousins were just waking up and stretching. I glanced at the extension before going indoors. I think they must have outdone themselves that day by falling asleep immediately upon arriving. None the less, by the end of the week, as they had assured us, they were ready for Neville the Traker to frame the roof. We wanted a few individual features in the interior. It was time for us to visit the Architectural Salvage Yard Henry had told us about.

The Yard had no signs or obvious indications of its presence. We only chanced upon it by returning on our second attempt with precise written directions from Henry. In order for an Architectural Salvage Yard to achieve maximum prices, it was necessary to persuade the customers that they had chanced upon the place themselves against all odds. The proprietor also had to persuade the customers with rude, unhelpful behaviour that the last thing he wanted to do was to sell any of his vast accumulation of items.

When we had negotiated the narrow entrance and the interminably long track which obviously had material regularly removed from it rather than added, we were faced by a vista of ancient relics and a scowling Drool who seemed most annoyed to see us. I told him that we wanted to look round, he grunted with a bend of the knees. I was sure he would rather have had us leave, but we were captivated. Trapped here, in this great forest clearing, were the quintessential parts of hundreds of fine Provender buildings. We were unsure whether our rude extension could seriously accommodate such polite architectural details, but we were prepared to try.

In one corner there were rows and rows of sundials, some even larger than ours, often with defaced numerals where the previous owners had tried to move the numbers, not the dial, to cope with Incontinent Continental Drift. In another part, enormous table tops of polished Couth rested on undressed Couth bases, left over from the age when the creatures who built the houses built in the furniture too in matching materials.

A covered building housed enormous Gagas, capable of cooking a herd of Nullion simultaneously, and various other ranges adapted for the cooking of individual species. They dated back to the times when the dead of Provender – provided they had had no taste-impairing complaint – were cooked and eaten by the remaining family as a matter of respect. Each species would have a special cooker suitable for cooking its own kind in a specially reserved corner of the kitchen. Standing in lines were Colwig cookers, Montalban cookers, all manner of shapes and sizes of cookers. We had heard that long ago a family of Conimunculi had gone completely native and had had a Conimunculi cooker constructed especially for them by Luigi Gaga, the founder of the famous firm. Thankfully, the practice had long since ceased. Another corner of the yard was reserved for early ablution suites of every shape and size, and varying degrees of danger. It was a hazardous task keeping clean in those days with the maze of pipes and scrapers that sprouted from them. My wife spotted, tucked away in a corner, an early gratification suite with wild Putrage growing from the harness.

We could not make our minds up. The choice of architectural features was astonishing. In one corner a hovering buttress was still aloft, tethered to a post. Elsewhere in jumbled piles were columns, entire double helix staircases and domes of various shapes clad in various materials, some of which were self-motivating. We took a close look at a complete Halmatrope cellar, carefully removed and placed on lumps of Couth, still with its slats and splat-backed sampling chair and drainage gully. Architectural styles and periods jostled together; collapsed Trake frames, half-jettied Drisk hovels; a broken pediment from a Palissandrian Nullion plumper and too much to ever take in one visit. The proprietor seemed pleased when we left his stock untouched and went home. I wondered if we could ever find the place again even if we wanted to. Perhaps it vanished as soon as we left.

When we arrived home we found that our ablution suite and gratification suite had finally arrived all the way from Conima. It was months since we had ordered them. We had expected to hear of their arrival from the Import Office, but an attached note stated that the punitive Import Tariff had been removed from our Credit Rating without our authority. To make matters worse, without even opening the case, we knew that the gratification suite was much too small and that the ablution suite was not the model we had ordered. I 'screened through to the supplier on Conima at great expense. He checked his records and said that the delivery code was identical to the order code. He could change the suites if they were unopened and charge us for the collection and delivery but the process would take another three months.

We went straight out for a meal to console ourselves. We knew just the place to visit. Each time we had been to the market we had smelt the delicious vapours coming out of its small unassuming doorway and had vowed to visit it. It was run by Spansules, there was little room inside, only four tables, but only one of them was occupied. Two Drools had brought their small son with them, he was loud and unruly. We ordered wild mulver steeped in Nullion skin secretions and Gormandine. We sipped an unusual little Halmatrope while we waited and the young Drool's behaviour worsened. He started whining for the ablution suite and his parents asked the Spansule waitress where it was. She pointed through a door and the young Drool rushed through it, never to be seen again. After some time had elapsed his mother went to look for him. She rushed back for her husband. They were gone for quite some time. Our mulver arrived and as we tried to savour it we were continually disturbed by comings and goings. I was going to have a word with the parents when we gathered from the outcry that the young Drool had been too small to use the ancient ablution suite and had disappeared through the grill. It was a salutary warning not to spoil other people's meals by bringing along offspring. We left without having our customary Algarglanon and returned to face our own ablution suite and gratification suite problem. They would probably have to stay. We might go through the whole process of ordering replacements and still get the wrong consignment.

Henry introduced us to his second cousin, Neville, a fifth-generation Traker, older than Henry. I asked him if he was familiar with the Dolbury Joint. 'Oh, yes,' he said, 'barefaced soffit tenons with diminished haunches and two-face pegs. Cost you extra of course.' I was impressed but I said we would settle for a standard job. He was disappointed. He measured and cut while Henry and his cousins assembled. They were given no opportunity to sleep while Neville worked. The roof followed through from the existing roofline. We had not taken much notice of our roofing material before. The pitch was quite low to diminish resistance to the winter's green vapours, so the covering was really only evident when looked down on from the hill above and then the tenacious foliage that sprouted on it made it blend in well with its surroundings. We asked Henry what it was.

'Split Splandrite,' he said, 'more durable than Couth.'

I asked him where it came from. Apparently millions of years ago when the galaxy's first advanced civilization, the Yolmi, developed the ultimate in fast food they discovered that the self-delivering burger containers damaged the atmosphere as they sped through to the customer. So they gathered them all together and contracted for their disposal. By chance, the entire load was dumped on Provender where it formed a third continent. The disposed containers immediately reacted with the higher atmospheric pressure and Noxule gas and hardened into a substance which was resistant to weather, yet supported life. It is all that remains of the Yolmi, as food became faster and faster so did their lives, until near the end they were thinking and communicating too fast for any other species to comprehend. Recordings were made of their final scientific conclusions before they vapourized but fast enough machines have not yet been developed to interpret and reveal this priceless knowledge. Instead, their packaging is extracted in great blocks of Splandrite and skilled splitters separate each layer. They are then fixed to roofs, face upwards, the original monogram on the front just visible when they are wet. Henry told us he had some second-hand Splandrite with a growth on to match ours. We were growing fond of Henry, he was building a fine extension in his own good time.

When the roof was finished, matching perfectly with the old roof, we felt that some form of celebration was deserved, even if the whole project was scarcely half finished. As Henry fixed the last Splandrite we brought out the Halmatrope and plates of cold Nullion with slices of Gormandine. We sat on the patio in the hot sun with our eyes barely open and the sounds of the baby Riticules in our ears on the sundial.

Henry turned up the next day with his plasterer to show him the job. He was quite young, short with long thin limbs, ending in long thin filaments.

'This is Lesley,' Henry said.

'Are you an Ochran?' I asked. He was; a tenth-generation Ochran. Yes, he said, his great grandfather probably had done Mr Skeg's ceiling and yes, he could do something similar for us, but it would cost extra. We left him to measure up and make notes. Henry took me aside.

'You know about Ochrans?' he asked in a hoarse whisper. Then he reminded me. They alternate sexes from day to day. Today he was male. He approached us.

100

'Tricky, but I can do something for you.' He spotted my wife and grinned broadly. 'Good day to you' he said, fixing her with a stare that made her blush.

'Start tomorrow, right?' he said to Henry, who nodded.

The next day Lesley turned up before Henry did. He spotted me as he daintily unloaded his tools and gave me such a lovely smile that I was quite taken aback until I remembered that Lesley would be female that day. When Henry and his cousins arrived Lesley flirted outrageously and got very little work done until they fell asleep in the afternoon. The next day Lesley cornered my wife in the kitchen and would not let her out until she kissed him, then later he picked a fight with Don.

The workmanship was exquisite but I wondered how long we could put up with Lesley. One day he would be a real nuisance to my wife, the next a real nuisance to me. Meanwhile, Henry and his cousins fitted the windows.

My wife and I walked up the hill one afternoon and were dismayed to see dozens of temporary structures in shockingly bright colours scattered among the trees. Now and again a head would appear through an opening, then retreat when we were spotted. Dorf, even on our hill now. Goodness knows what they were eating. The hill was quiet otherwise. Usually as we walked we could hear creatures scuttling away through the undergrowth at every step, but not that day.

We passed Mr Skeg. 'Dorf,' he grunted, 'we should Instamort them all. Still, they'll be gone by tomorrow, you'll see. Eat what they can and go. Probably ate your Pallions,' he added with a twitch, and carried on home.

We said nothing to each other on the way home. Somehow, we both knew that we would never see our Pallions again, whether or not we had the Dorfs to blame.

AUGUST

We had been warned how hot August could be in Provender. It was too hot to venture out at all in the middle of the day and most things became too hot to touch. Henry and his cousins worked short mornings, beating holes through into the original part of the house and then drove home to fall asleep. It was time for George, the plumber, to start. He began in the extension, fitting his pipework in each room before Lesley plastered the walls. He tried hard to avoid Lesley but inevitably he would find himself having to fight Lesley off for one reason or another. He rushed through the extension pipework and refused to come back until Lesley had finished completely. I questioned Henry about Lesley's marital status. He was indeed married. It was a simple process, Ochrans sought out partners whose sexual cycle opposed theirs and enjoyed deep and long-lasting relationships, while none the less retaining a fascination for other species.

We had decided that, when George came back to finish the heating system and fit our ablution suite, we would have the Noxule gas system, with all its drawbacks. We were not going to be forced to pay ridiculous prices for solar power. Just after we had made this decision, coincidentally we heard a knock on the door. I opened it and, standing in the midday heat, totally unaffected, was a smoothly presented Dorf. He introduced himself and showed me his card. Aha, I thought, not a tourist, but a salesman. Did we have central heating? he asked. We said no. Were we planning to have any? We said yes. Which sort? Noxule gas, we said. He laughed. It was a studied controlled laugh. Had we considered nuclear power? he asked. We laughed, rather hysterically, I thought later.

'Ah, wait a minute,' he said. 'You've been taken in by all the bad publicity of the past.' We had to admit we had.

'Now,' he said, 'nuclear power is cheaper than ever. Pay nothing today and defer your payments until later.' He told us that his company from Manufex would install the unit for no cost at all. Then we would have cheap clean power for ten years. Then what? we said.

'Oh, who can look ahead that far?' he chuckled, good-naturedly.

Then I remembered the trick. They had tried it on Conima years ago. You get your free unit, cheap power for ten years, then you have to pay them a fortune to remove it and until they do your house is worthless and you have a Hazardous Zone Confinement Order placed on you. I showed him to the door and watched with great relief as his Stromba grated off down the drive, sparking now and again on the bumps. I hoped that no creature in the vicinity would be taken in.

The roads around Bepommel were busy now. The Palissandrians descended on their holiday homes in August and the prices went up in the markets and the restaurants and all the artisans rushed to do their bidding at extortionate prices. We had reached another impasse on the extension. George would not finish his plumbing until Lesley had finished the plastering and Henry could not finish until Lesley finished. Lesley, in the meantime, was carrying out some emergency *trompe-l'oeil* plasterwork for some Palissandrians. We wondered how they would react to Lesley. Perhaps they had a plasterer every vacation.

There were several Palissandrian holiday lodges beyond Mr Dobson's and we chanced to meet a couple walking on the hill in the early evening. They said they were having a party the next evening for their Palissandrian friends who were staying in the vicinity and would we like to come. We could imagine what a formal affair it was likely to be, but Palissandrians always provided good food and drink, so we said we would love to come.

The next evening we took the Stromba up to their lodge and found a secluded spot to hide it before passing all the lined-up Ferenziculos, Masquerandis and other exotic vehicles I had never even heard of. Our hosts, Melissa and Rupert, greeted us at the door. We were the only Conimunculi and we felt a little ill at ease. It was so long since we had worn our best clothes that even after letting them fully out they were conspicuously too small. We were offered Halmatrope. I glimpsed the bottle and felt dizzy, the 22406! How had they ever got hold of it? And then to offer it to guests without comment. I saw new arrivals after us take the Halmatrope and drain it during conversation without a thought. We were in a dilemma, should we creep away into a corner and savour it to the last drop or socialize and try to make the best of it?

The choice was taken away from us when our host, thinking that we were shy, ushered us over to meet Dr Dilsby and his wife. He was an old Palissandrian now, the last remaining living member of the galactically famed scientific team that carried out the relative relativity experiments. Dr Dilsby had been a junior member of the team that developed the Luminule. This was a capsule containing measuring devices and two scientists which had been developed with the capacity to exceed the speed of light. The purpose was to pursue a light particle, overtake it and see how it behaved. The experiment was a failure. As the Luminule gathered speed in the cyclotron at the precise moment that it overtook the light particle, all the lights went out in its cabin and the scientists could not see a thing until they had slowed down again. It was remarkable to be in the same room as a creature of such renown, let alone be introduced to him. Strangely, as is often the case with great creatures, he was modest and seemed far more interested in hearing about me than discussing his life, which I did give him an opportunity to do, early on.

A magnificent buffet was laid on. When we were called through we just did not know where to start, there was even a section of 'Fresh Food' carefully enclosed so nothing could escape. We decided to try some. We stepped in and I seized a pair of little creatures in spikey shells and gave one to my wife. We watched the Palissandrian next to us. He opened his mouth wide, tipped his head back as far as it would go then held the shell above and gave it a sharp rap with a piece of Trake. I tried it and the creature leapt out of its shell with the shock of the knock and straight into the welcoming shelter of my mouth. I swallowed hard and felt it wriggle and slither all the way down my throat. It was delightful, a true gastronomic experience, and the after-taste was superb.

When everyone had finished we expected them to form into small groups and earnestly debate but not a bit of it. They obviously preferred to leave their Palissandrian customs behind and adopt the local ones. Jackets came off, ties were loosened from around etiolated necks and low-frequency vibration music replaced the dainty high-frequency background sounds that accompanied the early part of the evening. Our hosts and their friends were transformed and, emulating Drools, they stomped and whirled around; some imitated Drisks to whoops of encouraging laughter, even Dr Dilsby did a passable Colwig which cleared the floor and sent everybody into a ring around him clapping. We suspected that if we had not been there someone might have danced like a Conimunculi but they were polite enough to leave us to carry out that embarrassing display ourselves.

We headed home exhausted in the early hours of the morning, leaving our hosts and their few remaining guests fast asleep. On the way into our drive the Stromba swung out too far turning into the garage and hit the new ablution suite, damaging its wing and shattering one of the suite's Molar ball and claw feet. We could not send it back now, even if we wanted to.

My friend from Conima, Mayhew, 'screened me. Could he come to stay? We had vaguely invited him months back to visit us in August, thinking that all our work would be finished. He was the galaxy's worst guest. He needed more space than most guests but we loved him. He said he would come as soon as he could. Three days later I received a 'screen from Mayhew. He was not at the Cosmodrome. He was not in Bepommel. He was not sure where he was, and could I pick him up?

It transpired that, at the Cosmodrome, Mayhew had leapt through an open door of a vehicle, thinking it was a taxi and slammed the door. When he noticed there was a passenger in the back seat already, another Conimunculi, he started chatting away in his usual affable manner. The driver assumed that the two passengers were acquainted and pulled off to his predetermined destination. The passenger naturally assumed that Mayhew had a right to be there as the driver had permitted him to stay. It was not until they pulled up outside Corto-Probax House in Nolbergale that Mayhew realized that he had not yet given the driver any directions. Then he discovered that the vehicle was a Corto-Probax chauffeured limousine for executives and it was not available for the two-hour drive to Bepommel with a non-executive, let alone a non-employee. By then the passenger had become an old friend and invited Mayhew in to use a 'screen and have a Halmatrope. Mayhew, unfortunately, had the Halmatrope first and then another and another and forgot about the 'screen and us. He and his friend left Corto-Probax House and decided to sample the cuisine of Nolbergale. They sampled one restaurant after another, losing track of time and eventually space. When Mayhew woke up in the early hours of the morning he was behind a restaurant wearing nothing but a Drisk suspender belt and some discreet pink material, possibly lent by two Copuli. His friend was nowhere to be seen and two bladderats were eyeing him suspiciously. With no means of identification, proof of Credit Rating or clothing it would not be easy to persuade the restaurant owner to let him use their 'screen. He stayed in hiding until he heard signs of life inside. They, of course, remembered him as soon as they saw him. One or two items of his clothing were scattered about the interior. Some creature had also handed in his wallet containing all his documents. It was then that he 'screened me. The Drisk restaurant proprietor helped fill out some details of how to find them and I set out on the two-hour journey with resignation. This was the least you could expect from a Mayhew visit. When I eventually found him he was in the sort of establishment we would not normally patronize but in Provender every new experience is valid. He was by now a lifetime friend of the proprietor and his wife, a rather sultry little Drisk who had no doubt provided Mayhew with the suspender belt. He insisted that he bought me a meal before we left. I had poor expectations of the quality of food there, but I could not refuse. We were provided with a house Halmatrope. It was dull and lifeless. I expected the same of the food, but when it came, I knew from the first steaming whiff that we were in for a treat. Mayhew thought so too.

'Never tasted anything like it,' he spluttered through a full mouth.

I had to agree and yet, we decided, there was none the less something familiar about it, a faint odour, the texture. I remembered my earlier vow, never to enquire. But Mayhew had made no such vow. As we prepared to leave he asked the proprietor what the food had been, he was sure he knew it, but could not place its name.

'You should do,' the proprietor replied in gruff

Spheraglese, 'you brought it with you.'

'Ah,' Mayhew said, and wisely decided to enquire no further while there was still an element of doubt.

We were totally dehydrated by the time we got home. The heat affected the Stromba too. It seemed unable to garage itself and kept bumping into the front of the garage before switching itself off and becoming too hot in the sun to touch. My wife was in the lagoon and we dived in ourselves with a sizzle as our bodies entered the water. Mayhew seemed unaffected by his night's activities and was all for going out that evening for a meal in Bepommel, but we thought it safer if we stayed home to eat.

My wife and I were preparing the evening meal when Mayhew came in from the lagoon. He had been relaxing in the Flasted 49. He said he fancied a quick walk up the hill to give himself an appetite. We were sure his appetite needed no encouragement but we warned him that the meal was almost ready as he sped out of the door. We should have known. Two hours later Mayhew appeared, just as we had decided to give up waiting for him. The Flasp was over-cooked and the Dandralobe was too brittle but Mayhew tucked in enthusiastically and was full of compliments.

'Just had a preprandial Halmatrope with your neighbours the Montalbans,' he said. 'Best stocked private cellar I've seen in ages. Nothing too fancy, just good reliable stuff. They know what they are up to those chaps.' We were amazed. 'They said you might be having a new neighbour soon.'

'Oh?' I replied. 'Is Mr Skeg going?'

'No, no, some Drool, had a lot of interest in his place.'

We had not even known Mr Dobson's house was on the market.

'Apparently Alaric Rincon is after a holiday home here.'

My wife and I looked at each other and winced: Rincon

was a style guru in Conima. His minions scoured the galaxy looking for unique items of furniture made individually in the finest materials so that he could copy them and mass produce them by the million in cheap materials and sell them in his Ecotat Store chain.

'Only interested, nothing definite,' he soothed.

I fetched the Algarglanon to take our minds off the subject. We relaxed sipping our Algarglanon and I broached another sensitive subject.

'How long are you staying then, Mayhew?'

He had been planning to spend two nights with us, but the first had inadvertently vanished in Nolbergale so this would be the only night he could spare. We breathed a sigh of relief as unobtrusively as possible and as he leaned back in his chair I heard something structural snap inside it. It lost all its shape and collapsed taking him down with it while his Algarglanon flew all over the room. He was most apologetic and diplomatically retired to bed while my wife and I spent half the night trying to soak out the Algarglanon from the rug before it permanently stained it. Our rug had been purchased on a holiday on Aspersasp, a mountainous planet covered in Halitoids. These are bulky creatures with tiny little feet. However, they are surprisingly agile and twirl and pirouette up and down near vertical rock faces. The local hill creatures trap the Halitoids once a year in the autumn, give them an antiseptic mouthwash and pluck the little springy hairs from their inside legs. They then spend the long winter nights weaving these hairs into the most luxurious, soft, springy rugs imaginable. We did not want ours indelibly stained.

To avoid any further problems we arranged the next morning for a taxi to take Mayhew to the Cosmodrome. He was full of apologies and gratitude as he shook our hands. He was impossible but once again we told him he was welcome any time.

SEPTEMBER

On alternate days my wife and then I would keep well out of the way. Lesley was back. I noted when he had gone in the evenings that one day he would plaster great smooth expanses of wall, the next he would add delicate tracery to a ceiling, or clusters of fruit, frozen in the pulverized, roasted and slaked material. Henry turned up to see how he was progressing. I did not envy Henry's role as employer.

'Just a few more days,' Henry told me, 'then we'll be back with Neville to carry on.' I noted he said 'carry on', and not, as I had hoped, 'finish off'. I 'screened George and told him that the house would be safe in a few more days. Perhaps he, at least, would soon be finished.

The area was quiet again now. The Palissandrians had all gone. Market and restaurant prices were cheaper again. The sun was still hot, but not quite so hot. Mr Dobson told us that two visitors must have hammered unsuccessfully on their big front door, probably at midday, a few weeks earlier. They never used the big front door themselves, only the small door at the back. The big front door had been shut when his wife's father was carried out and never opened since. When they happened to walk past it in the evening they noticed their visitors, who I later heard were an estate agent with a prospective purchaser, were fried to a crisp. It had been a good summer. Mr Dobson also mentioned that soon he would be releasing the Halmatrope spores. They were late this year. Then would come the bottling. We could hardly wait. In the meantime Mr Dobson was concerned about the weather.

'Be a storm tonight,' he warned. 'I can feel it in my juices.'

Drools had a tube that ran round one of their legs that responded to barometric pressure, swelling and pulsing as the pressure dropped. 'Shame the Putrage is late this year. A storm this time of year can ruin the crop.'

Sure enough, we were woken up in the night by foam roaring overhead, squeezing torrentially everywhere, and the sky was rent and set alight by enormous explosions of Noxule gas ignited by the piezoelectrical discharge from the drifting continents. Glad that the extension was weather-proof now, we could hear things crashing about outside as the storm intensified. Suddenly there was one enormous crash. I rushed to the window and peered out. When the sky was lit up by the next explosion I saw our Flasted 49 had been flung through the air and had landed on the new grati-fication suite which was still waiting to be fitted.

The next morning when we woke up the sky was clear again and the sun was hot, but all down the valley we could see the damage of the night before. Trake had been uprooted and our drive had been half washed away, but the Putrage seemed undamaged.

Lesley was giggly and bashful on the last day of plas-tering. There was a little tidying up and one or two finishing touches to the clusters of Hollombrost and Matchagan, which seemed real enough to pluck, in spite of their lack of colour. We offered her a celebratory Halmatrope and she sat and gossiped with my wife and flashed her eyes at me. We thanked her profusely for the craftsmanship but when she wiggled back to her vehicle and drove off in a cloud of dust we were so relieved we had an impromptu snack of Ansate which had been left to hang in the kitchen for just such an occasion.

The next day Henry and his cousins turned up to work on the fireplace, followed by Neville to hang the doors. Soon after George arrived. I took him aside and explained our decision to have a Noxule gas system. He was not surprised he said, he had noted our resolve not to be penalized by arbitrary tax regimes. He said he always kept a stock of all the fittings necessary, although it might take several trips to bring them over, owing to their bulky nature. We had also decided that the Noxule system, although obtrusive, was more in keeping with a vernacular cottage, although we were a little dismayed when George told us that the only suitable place for the tank was in the front of the house, obscuring the view of the lagoon. It was a regulation he said, as Henry and his cousins were easing the tank on to its Couth plinth, that tanks had to be kept near standing water for when they caught fire. Henry guffawed. I was perturbed by his use of 'when' instead of 'if', but it was obviously all part of the charm of vernacular systems that they had their little foibles.

George examined the damaged ablution suite. He could sort something out, he said. It was not as easy to repair as Molarite, but something could be done. At the same time he cast his eye over the gratification suite. Henry and his cousins had lifted the Flasted 49 off and carried it back to the pool, where it sank. They had not noticed the hole in the base. They moved the gratification suite indoors before opening the crate. George told us the rotary arm was repairable but he was unfamiliar with the probe and sensor filaments, or the rest of it. I would have to call in an expert from Palissandria.

'That sounds expensive,' I said. He nodded.

Mr Dobson dropped by in the afternoon to warn us that the hunting season was to begin the next day. It only lasted a week and was principally aimed at the large tasty Cutlings, but everything else was at risk too. The Cutling is almost totally meat. Instead of evolving a better shape to move fast and avoid its predators, as it evolved it kept its original shape and developed enormous amounts of muscle on top of it to overcome its earlier inefficiencies. This made it faster but a much better proposition to eat, thus it focused more attention on itself rather than less.

In the morning we were woken by the sounds of pursuit. We kept off the hill that week. The Cutling may be wonderful to eat with sprigs of Brotch, but to chase it with a pointed Trake seems a trifle barbaric, when all you need to do is leave a couple of Halmatrope out for it then spray it with Instamort while it sleeps.

We went to Bepommel for provisions and discovered that it was the day of the annual Clovis races. When we had stocked up the Stromba we followed everybody to the side street where the race was to be. We had often wondered why creatures kept Clovis. The flesh was pleasant enough but unremarkable considering the amount of care and attention the Clovis required. Even more care and attention was required for the Fainting Clovis, the hybrid used for street racing. At some point in its evolutionary cycle a male Clovis decided that, instead of trying to knock another Clovis senseless with its large thick head in order to win a female, there might perhaps be a simpler way. He tried fainting. The other males shrank away in case it was catching and the females crowded in to help. His numerous resulting offspring inherited this tendency, with one drawback, eventually they had no control over when they fainted. This gave Clovis racing an element of chance. If the Clovis did not faint at all it was disqualified, thus eliminating imposters. We joined the lines of Bepommel inhabitants along the street. At the far end of the street the Clovis were lined up ready. One fainted before the race had even started but it had come to by the time the race was on and the owners had let them go. A brownish one raced straight into the lead, then passed out tripping up the two Clovis just behind it, one of which fainted as it fell. The Drool next to me roared encouragement at the Clovis as the race shot past. He had placed a bet on it, but it fell again just before the end. The first one to cross the line was disqualified for not fainting at all, it had scarcely even run, and the winner stumbled groggily over the line, obviously not quite sure where it was. It was greeted with tumultuous applause and promptly fainted again. Its owner had to take it away on a trolley. After this edifying experience we drove home slowly appreciating the views. We were beginning to feel that we had lost our home. Artisans would casually wander in and out, some days they would all turn up, some days none of them would. We kept telling ourselves that it would all be over soon but then nobody turned up for a week.

We decided, to pass the time waiting for the work to be finished, that we would drive out to the Trake woods and select our own bark. I asked Mr Skeg's advice. He cackled. 'I said you'd be getting your own. Didn't I say?' We drove back with the Stromba boot full and set about hanging the bark to dry in the kitchen. The kitchen was always full of Hully flies so the next stage of the process was guaranteed to progress.

Mr Dobson visited. He had organized some help and the next day the Halmatrope would be released, weather permitting, but his juices were not too optimistic. I asked him how the hunting had gone.

'Shocking,' he said. 'Only caught a little skinny sick one. The Dorfs must have got the rest.'

The following day was glorious, in spite of Mr Dobson's earlier misgivings. By the time we emerged he and his helpers were halfway across the jostling Putrage, flinging little puffs of Halmatrope spores up into the air to flutter down on it. They worked their way across and then flung any left-over spores as far as they could back into the Putrage. Mr Dobson called them in. It was obviously part of the ritual. They all stood in a ring and had one of the previous year's Halmatrope then sang a song. They sang on and off all the rest of the morning, marching round the edge of the Putrage singing in some ancient dialect we could not understand. Mr Dobson told us later that they were singing to the Halmatrope, telling it to eat its fill and grow strong and full of juice, wishing it health and flavour and hoping it would take to its new home, the bottle. Then they all sat at the end of the Putrage where they had started, and tucked into a fine meal prepared and brought out to them by Mrs Dobson. The sun beat down and for the first time we noticed that the Putrage had stopped moving. On its stems little swollen creatures were visible where the leaves had been. Mr Dobson walked around inspecting. He went back to sit down nodding confidently. An old Zulex bumped up to them, full of bottles. Mr Dobson carefully finished the last morsels of his meal, stood and stretched, then gave the order and all of them got up and seized bottles. They worked their way across, popping every Halmatrope they could see individually into a bottle. Some brought empty bottles along, some filled, some took the full bottles away. Years of co-operation allowed them to work smoothly singing another song to the tiny Halmatrope, urging it to grow and fill its bottle. It was almost dark when the last bottle was filled and the Zulex slowly hauled the load back to one of Mr Dobson's outbuildings. He sat down and mopped his brow and opened a Halmatrope. We had watched on and off all day. We went over to ask him how it had gone.

'Marvellously,' he said, standing up obviously still enthused by the day's success. 'That is to say,' he elaborated, 'not quite as bad as expected. I expect half of them won't grow to fill their bottles, we just chuck them away then. Still,' he grinned lopsidedly, 'I'll try and find a few good bottles for you, don't you worry, even if we get none ourselves.'

'Oh, don't deprive yourself after all your hard work,' I said, and he nodded and chuckled and said he would not.

Mr Malvern travelled all the way from Palissandria to look at our gratification suite. We had discussed the matter first on the 'screen and I noticed a slightly sarcastic tone, but gave him the benefit of the doubt. He obviously knew only too well that we had little choice but to use him, unless we brought in an expert from Conima at even greater expense.

My earlier suspicions were confirmed. Mr Malvern told us immediately that we should have ordered our suite through him. He asked us if we had ordered that particular model, the Nirvana Sensulex. We had to admit that it was not our intended purchase, but we had decided to make do with it. He snorted and examined the damaged rotary arm with a critical fingertip.

'Pleasure is a serious business, you know.' He lectured us sternly. 'Did you sit on it or something?' he asked. I was becoming rather irritated with his attitude. I informed him that at no time in the past had my wife or I sat on the rotary arm, nor did we intend to at any point in the future. We were fully cognizant of the correct use of the rotary arm, we just wanted it fixed and the filaments overhauled. He went to his vehicle and returned with an assortment of spare parts and equipment.

An hour later he barged in on us in the kitchen and said he had replaced the arm and rehung the filaments. It was time to calibrate. I said we would calibrate it ourselves. He said it was madness to bring him all that way without calibrating it, particularly as we were Conimunculi, he added, rudely, I thought. Then, noting that we were insistent on that point, he suggested that it should at least be tested once in his presence and if we would not, perhaps he should. We agreed to that but pointed out that there was as yet no door. He seemed unperturbed.

Mr Malvern was in a better mood when he reappeared, several hours later. We offered him a snack before he set off on his long journey back. He assured us that the suite was now in perfect working order. We noticed that he was a little wobbly on his legs as we accompanied him to his vehicle and saw him off.

Now all we needed was for the rest of the work to be finished.

OCTOBER

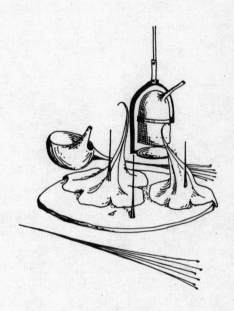

My wife and I were walking in the hills early one morning. The sky was clear, save for one or two meteors exploding with a puff in the upper atmosphere. We looked down on our house now doubled in size. The gas tank was something we would have to come to terms with and the new roof was a slightly different colour, but as close a match of surface foliage as could be expected. The areas of Putrage behind were strangely still, stripped of their leaves by the Halmatrope. Mr Dobson had told us that it would be a month or two before the new leaves grew large enough to harness the solar energy which activated them.

There was very little to do to finish the work, or so it seemed to us. A few small awkward jobs were left, some tidying up and repairs to the inevitable damage caused by the whole protracted process. We had considered suggesting to Henry that instead of calling himself a building contractor, he might consider building protractor more appropriate, but we decided it would lose its effect in Spheraglese. There was also the problem of finding Henry in the first place to tell him.

We reached a lightly wooded area of hill and stopped suddenly. There, under a dense bush, legs were visible sprawled on the moist ground. We initially thought something was dead but as we approached to investigate the creature cried, 'Aha,' shot upright and backed out of the bush carrying a large, long white fleshy thing. He was shocked when he turned and saw us and we realized that he was an old Drisk.

'You've got to be early to get these beauties fresh,' he croaked. We asked him what it was.

'This one? It's a Nullion Podge, that's what we calls 'em

125

anyways. Looks just loike one, doesn't it?' He laughed dirtily. 'Acterly, all these are Glandaloops, all different shapes and sizes. You're touring, are you?'

'Certainly not,' I said, 'we live here.'

'Oh. I'd have thought you knew what they was then. This time o' year, in the early morning they pops up everywhere, but if you don't pick 'em then, they shrivels up again by midday, no flavour then.' He walked on through the trees and bushes, then stopped. A heap of leaves was twitching. 'There,' he said, handing us the Glandaloop, 'that's what you look for.' He knelt down by the leaves. We heard a sort of grunting sound. Something was making a big effort. Then there was a most unpleasant smell and a Glandaloop slightly smaller and darker than the one in my hand burst through the leaves, almost hitting the old Drisk on the head. He plucked it straight up.

'Oh, these are tasty, these darker ones. Mind, those are not so bad neither. You take him, you try him,' he said, pointing to the one we were holding.

'You can eat them raw, but I prefers them grilled both sides in a dab of smolene for ten minutes. The sooner you pick 'em, the better they taste. You can't get no fresher than these.'

We were fascinated. We thanked the old Drisk and walked home, carrying our breakfast. We followed his recommendations but he should have warned us. Once well chewed and swallowed and the marvellous taste savoured, all is not over. It seems to rise slowly back up to the mouth of its own volition, then it tastes quite different, but still delicious as you swallow it again. Then the process repeats itself, and again and again, each time tasting different but delightful. After an hour or so of unrelenting delight we were still without nutrition and feeling extremely hungry despite our temporarily full stomachs. We decided there was only one solution, we had to spit it out. This, I later learned, was the correct procedure. With Glandaloops in

126

season, stalls on the market were soon stocked with them and restaurants were serving them, with spitoons available.

We had a rather battered set of the Encyclopedia Galactica. We punched in for the Glandaloop to see just what it was. Apparently, the Cthon, a slow boring, or possibly slow, boring, creature lives just below the surface consuming microscopic pocrobes all year long. It then excretes Glandaloops once a year. Once again, we should have resisted the temptation to enquire more closely. The Encyclopedia is rather too sketchy on Provender in general. It was then, as now, considered of little importance in the Galaxy. All these things are relative: I have been told by those who have visited the great library of Knoall which occupies its entire planet, that they possess the Galaxy's only copy of the prohibitively expensive Encyclopedia Universalis, which spins around the planet separately twice a day in the form of an artificial satellite. This rates our Galaxy as scarcely worth a mention. It never hurts to keep things in proportion. Such a massive store of knowledge can be rather daunting. Only the longest living creatures could read even a fraction of the 'A' entries. Dinner parties the galaxy over are littered with small groups of creatures arguing heatedly and knowledgeably over a broad range of topics. It is only if you listen closely that you realize that they all begin with 'A'. There are a few dissident groups of intellectuals but you will find that all their discussions boil down to 'Z'.

We have recently found a secondhand copy of the Galatony Guide to Provender restaurants on a market stall. There are few highly recommended establishments in our vicinity; none the less, there are copious notes on less formal institutions of the sort which we visit regularly.

Colpoise Galatony was himself a chef of outstanding accomplishment before his tragic premature death in a 'Fresh House' with a party of Dorfs. He had several establishments in Palissandria but he was not afraid to venture

127

out in search of inspiration; each time he did he made notes, thus his guide began. He is amusing and complimentary about Bepommel, but he does not name any establishments actually in the town. We found references to the converted Drib Mill and the Copuli's establishment, which does not in fact mention that it is run by Copuli, an oversight I thought. There is also mention of a floating restaurant downstream from Bepommel. We had not heard of it. It specializes in cooking whatever its nets catch from the river as it rushes past. There is never a fixed menu, sometimes you get a treat, sometimes nothing special, but the well-stocked river always yields something up. We decided to pay it a visit.

We followed the directions in the guide and discovered a little track down by the river where a broad bend allowed the restaurant to float on relatively still water on the outer side while the rest of the river rushed through its nets on the inner side. The restaurant was built on the hull of an old Splandrite barge. In the early days, the split Splandrite would be brought as far inland as possible before being unloaded for local building works. We walked down the gangplank and were greeted by a Razmoth called Justin who wore some kind of old seafaring gear. He gripped us both firmly in welcome one after the other with his gripper and then showed us to our table. It was formed from the remains of a gigantic shell crimplet. Justin told us that it had been caught in the nets years ago and had been too bitter for most people's taste. Quite a few species tend to become a little bitter as they grow older. Other tables were formed from the residue of other meals: piles of Zoab ribs sewn together with gut; the skin of a Gaspa stretched over its lower mandibles; the knee cap of a fossilized MegaMega which had twirled by in a storm, washed down from some upriver deposits. Justin left to raise the net. He returned with a transparent tank on a trolley. This was to be our meal. We looked at it. It was full of creatures squirming and writhing in the cloudy water. If we could make our selection, Justin said, they would return the rest into the river.

'Selection?' we said. 'Just grill the lot.'

He wheeled the trolley out and shortly after a young Drool brought us mulled Halmatrope in a jug with tiny slices of Water Grudge. The waiter assured us it was the real thing. They had chanced to catch it the day before and removed it for general consumption.

Our plates arrived. The food was beautifully prepared and arranged. We had only been eating for half an hour when I saw my wife wince with pain. She told me it was her arm again, an old repetitive stress disorder. The amount of strain a particularly good meal can place on the body is often underestimated. In Conima, Restaurant Rescue Services used to be kept on standby to massage away mid-meal aches and pains, firmly pop back dislocated jaws and release the blockages that can so spoil a good meal out. I called Justin over. He was apologetic. There was nothing to be done. He had taken his Emeticist Certificate, compulsory for Provender restaurant managers, but he had never attended the advanced course. This cast a slight shadow on the evening, but my wife valiantly fought on and finished only an hour after me and never complained once about the pain. Justin offered us both a Dribui on the house. This remarkable drink is formed by leaving Algarglanon in vats of Drib for ten years then bottling it immediately. After a further ten years it is released from the bottle and it generally hits the ceiling with enough force to knock itself out and tenderize itself in one go. The taste is sublime.

When I heard a tap at the door one morning my first thought was 'Ah, the workmen at last,' but then I remembered that they had long since given up knocking. I opened the door and was confronted by a Spansule. He asked after my health and my family. I assured him that my wife was in fine health, save the odd twinge during mealtimes. Then he asked me if I realized that the planet was going to end. I said yes, I had grasped that it would not last for ever. 'Oh, no,' he said, did I realize that it was going to end on the last day of the year?

'Good gracious,' I said, 'as soon as that? How sad.'

Then he asked me if I wanted to be saved. I said not to bother and tried to shut the door, but his tail was wedged firmly in it. He said he had the answer, he had been told it and it was his duty to tell me. I asked him if it involved food and deftly kicked his tail aside. He said no, and thrust a foot in its place. 'How about drink then?' I asked, stamping on his foot. 'No,' he said, retracting his foot by reflex. 'I'm not interested then, thank you,' I said, managing to get the door shut. We were well used to prophecies of doom on Conima. Most of them were right. One week they would be saying 'Change your ways or the sea will die', the next week it was dead. One week they would tell us our soil would be sterile, the next week it was. No doubt the doors of Guspage were being hammered on repeatedly the evening before the asteroid hit it, but somehow I felt Provender had a good deal of life left in it yet.

I told Mr Dobson about our visitor when I saw him on the hill the next day. He said there was a simple way to discourage them, keep a sharpened Cutling Trake by the door. I asked him how the Halmatrope were growing. He fluttered his arms at waist level, 'So, so.' I asked if we could have a look. 'Not a good idea,' he said. 'Mustn't disturb them, later maybe, later.' Then he changed the subject. He said his wife's father was buried under our putrage which was why it had such a special significance to them. I was surprised, ground burial having long since died out on most planets. The case of Xin 16 was often cited in debates. The inhabitants all insisted on being buried in a modest plot of land. As millennia went by the population grew, less and less land was available to live on and more and more required for the dead. In the final years several tragic stampedes of the panicky population in their confined space killed enough of them to require the final land mass for graves. The residue was flown off to a small moon and only allowed back now and then to leave flowers. I mentioned Xin 16 to Mr Dobson.

'Birth control,' he said, 'that solves the burial problem. Sound birth control and you can have a decent burial.'

That reminded me of the planet Almarmara whose Supreme Leader the Worshipful Grand Polyp was an amorphous asexual voluble vegetable which discovered it could emit a mind-numbing vapour when stimulated by enormous crowds of Almarmarons. It had fallen off the back of a pan-galactic food transporter and was surrounded by crowds of Almarmarons as soon as it hit the ground. Then, to its surprise, it emitted the vapour which seemed to numb the crowds into submission and obedience. Sadly, the power soon went to its nuclei and it began assembling enormous crowds of Almarmarons, emitting its vapour and dictating edicts. It wanted greater and greater crowds to stimulate it, over and over, to produce more and more mind-numbing gas. It told them to multiply and that no means should be sought to inhibit their multiplication. They obeyed, but cried out for food, they were starving. 'Don't die,' it said, 'just breed.' Other neighbouring planets gave them food and they bred and bred and could not disobey it by dying. Soon the planet's surface was covered 10,000 deep in breeding Almarmarons, but still the Worshipful Grand Polyp urged them to breed and still it emitted more and more mind-numbing gas until, one day, it died peacefully in its sleep after a long and happy life. The gas was no longer emitted, the Almarmarons' brains began to function again and they looked around and asked, 'How, how could we allow an asexual vegetable to influence us in this way?' But it was too late. Suddenly the planet imploded under the enormous weight of Almarmarons and shrank to the size of a pill.

'Where did you hear all that?' Mr Dobson asked.

'I used to travel,' I said. 'You pick up an enormous amount of information travelling.'

131

'Yes,' said Mr Dobson. 'The knack is to know when to put it down again.'

George was the first of our missing artisans to return. He worked hard for two days bringing in the great heat emitters and connecting them up in each room. They were more intrusive than we had expected and George warned us not to put anything too close to them when they were working. On the third day he worked for a few hours and then told us that it was time to start the burner, but the gas tank had still not been filled. We had been waiting weeks for the tanker to visit. George shrugged and left.

We fought back our mounting frustration with a snack. In the kitchen the Hully flies had been taking great interest in our Trake bark. Several lumps had fallen from the ceiling under their weight. Mr Skeg had not warned us of their intensity and we wondered how the Robusta would ever get close enough to eat the eggs, if indeed there were any under the thick mat of flies.

The day the Noxule gas tanker arrived we also received a long-awaited delivery from Palissandria of material for the festoon blinds. My wife had ordered it from the Flora Diraea collection, imported from Conima by Deverell. Flora had pioneered the first of many quasi-nostalgia booms in Conima. While the population struggled under the weight of a collapsing civilization, fraught with new and ever more horrifying incurable diseases, Flora evoked a gentle bright past where diseases were merely controllable colourful embroideries on the fabric of life. She developed a material that would trap hosts of tiny parasites in pleasing wriggling patterns of bright colours. Her spring Epidemic Collection spread like wildfire, so that soon at least one room in every home in the land had it. Something that had first hatched out

132

on her kitchen table caught on everywhere. When the Conimunculi developed an immunity to it, other planets caught on and each year the potential market in the galaxy has extended exponentially. The Company slogan is indisputable: 'Flora Diraea will run and run'. This confirms that nostalgia for an imaginary past which never existed is a common trait in all beings with Credit Ratings above C.

The evenings were beginning to get noticeably cooler and we saw a Capricep turning up on our doorstep most evenings, just as it grew dark. My wife started giving it tiny leftovers from our meals and soon we felt that it had adopted us. Capriceps are as tasty as all other Provender creatures, but, somehow, they have managed to enshroud themselves in superstition. Provender Superstition has it that black Capriceps are lucky and black Capriceps with seventeen nipples are luckier still. As ours lay on its back to be tickled I counted: seventeen. Needless to say, the consumption of a seventeen-nippled Capricep was deemed to be most unlucky, not least for the Capricep. We had taken to it, just as it had taken to us. Superstition played no part in this. We would look after our Capricep as long as it wanted us to.

NOVEMBER

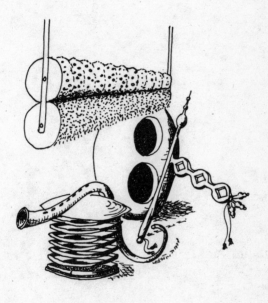

We were woken early by the 'screen. It was a rather sulky female Drisk. She said she had been given our name earlier by her employer, Coghlin Prawl. I said I had never heard of him. She said she looked after his holiday home. Something clicked. 'Is he by any chance an Image Transmuter?' I asked. She thought it was possible. She had turned up to change the atmosphere as she always did once a week in empty holiday homes and found him diamond buttoning a *chaise-longue*. Thinking the worst she had contacted us. I had to tell her that there was really nothing we could do, nothing any of us could do. I did not want to actually mention IDS. I told her she should quietly let herself out. My mind raced back over the events of his brief stay with us but I was quite sure that neither my wife nor I had, at any point, had a free and frank exchange of views with him. But what a surprise, obviously somebody had.

The kitchen was almost unusable now. The Hully flies seethed in masses over the disintegrating Trake bark and underneath the eggs seemed to be hatching. The process was a disaster. We would have no home-made infusion this year. Sadly, my wife and I Instamorted as many flies as we could and put them in the ice room, then we cleared up the mess and threw it outside away from the house into the bushes.

George appeared unexpectedly. We had left a message with his wife some days earlier telling him that the first gas delivery had come. He asked us if we had checked the tank. We said we knew nothing about it.

'Then you will have been short gassed by the driver,' he

said, 'and he will probably have given you second-grade gas, full of impurities unless you asked him. Well, don't blame me if anything goes wrong.'

I told George that we would indeed blame him. This made the first ignition of the system a fraught affair. George lifted the burner manifold, turned on all the gas valves, clicked his flamer and . . . a broad flame of gas licked around the burner and scorched the new ceiling. He slammed down the manifold cover and the flame roared on underneath, now, it seemed, safely confined. George grinned. 'There you are, went first time.' He said nothing about the smoking ceiling, but instead raced around the house turning all the heat emitters on. Then he said he had to be off to another job and not to touch anything. He would be back later.

Taking him at his word, we were forced to leave the house after two hours when the heat became unbearable. We opened all the windows and moved all our furniture as far away from the heat emitters as we could. Then we sat outside and persuaded our Capricep, whom we had called 'Tudor', to join us. We waited for George to return and took it in turns to race in for snacks to keep us going. George arrived in the early evening. He said he was pleased with the system's performance. He turned the system down and said that he would be back to check it again in a few days. We thanked him and he raced off. This left us to track down Henry and his various associates. The end of the year was approaching and we wanted everything finished.

We visited Henry's home the next day. His wife told us he was working on the other side of town and would be home late. Eventually we persuaded her to give us the directions there on the pretext that we had more work to offer him. This was not entirely untrue, there was the ceiling above the burner to repair.

The directions Henry's wife had given us were not very reliable. It was obviously not Henry's intention that his wife should find him in a hurry. Very few streets in Bepommel have names. A few have directional names, like North Street, but, due to the Incontinent Continental Drift, there are a number of North Streets established at different periods in Provender's history, none of which are justified in retaining the title. Very few houses have names or numbers in Bepommel either, and those that do have often chosen a number for sentimental or superstitious reasons. Seventeen is generally deemed to be a lucky number so in Bepommel there is a whole street full of number seventeens. This is a desirable neighbourhood and prices for property are high; a prospective purchaser should not, however, rate prompt delivery of goods or discovery by visitors high on their list of requirements.

The directions we had been given took us to an area of Palissandrian holiday homes. These took no note of local styles. They were bright, light and used artificial materials. We wondered what Henry, a vernacular artisan, could find to do. We spotted his Zulex parked outside a glittering glazed orb that slowly rotated on a delicate but immensely strong shiny spike. It was obviously not a metal found on Provender. We pulled up behind the Zulex. I could hear laughter inside the orb: Henry's rumbling chuckle and a thin, high giggle. It stopped as soon as the Stromba shut its doors. Then there was not a sound, but the orb seemed to quiver a little. It was another of those houses with no obvious door which Palissandrians in particular seem to love. It puts their guests or visitors at a loss from the outset. They can watch you make a complete idiot of yourself trying to get in and then graciously open up when it suits them. The most prestigious restaurant in Palissandria is built on these lines. It has no name. In the street outside there are no doors and no indication that there is any restaurant there at all. Those fortunate enough to gain admission sit at the mirrored windows and shriek with glee as well-known creatures try to gain entry, often unsuccessfully. Even if they do deign to admit you, once inside you are ignored completely

139

and have to find your way through a maze of unmarked corridors to the eating area. Once there, it is possible that you will never be served. The establishment is run, most profitably, by a behavioural psychologist who monitors the whole proceedings from a control room and makes spot decisions on how to treat each customer. If they get served at all they feel so privileged that they would never dream of complaining about the food which is brought in from a cheap little restaurant that backs on to it.

We were sure that Henry and some other creature were watching us as we stood outside and I was sure I heard a suppressed giggle.

'This is most unsatisfactory,' I said to my wife as we drove off. 'How can we ever get the work finished? What more can we do?'

My wife was pensive on the way back home. Then she said, 'We must have a party. Invite all the artisans and their wives to a party to celebrate the completion of the work at the end of the year. Then they'll have to finish it.'

I looked at my wife. 'You know, I think that could just do the trick.' We rushed in for a snack.

The next day Henry turned up early, on his own. I told him we had been looking for him. He seemed surprised. He said his Zulex had broken down and he had had to park it in someone's drive.

'That's twice your thoroughly reliable Zulex has let you down,' I observed, perhaps a little cruelly. He grinned feebly. He said he had come to make a list of the remaining jobs so he could get everything finished. My wife went to get a celebratory Halmatrope at these words. I sat Henry down.

'Another thing,' I said in my best Spheraglese. 'We want you, and all your artisans and their wives and all who have helped and delivered and supplied things, to come and eat and drink with us in a party to celebrate the end of everything, on the last day of the year.' He looked at me and I'm sure I spotted a tear in his eye.

'Surely not?' he said, stroking Tudor, who had leapt on to his lap.

'No, no, we are most insistent.'

'We couldn't,' he said.

'You must come and all the others. We'll supply the food.'

'So you say,' he said doubtfully.

'All you have to do is get it all finished. Then we can all celebrate.'

My wife brought in the Halmatrope and we shared a toast. 'To the house and its completion.'

Then Henry looked around the house making notes. I stopped him before he left.

'Oh, and if you could give the gratification suite priority: we've been waiting all this time for the door and the extractor fan.'

'Haven't you used it yet?' he asked, surprised.

'We are not going to calibrate it without even a door,' I snapped. 'Different creatures have different attitudes to gratification suites and Conimunculi have a code of behaviour, no matter where in the galaxy, or the universe, they may find themselves.'

Henry left, promising his prompt attention.

We were enjoying a meal of the last of the Hully flies with some Brotch when George burst in to check the heating system. He seemed satisfied. I asked him if he had heard about our proposed party. He said Henry had told him, he could not believe it.

'Why certainly,' I said, 'and you and your wife will be honoured guests as the first to finish here.'

He asked who would be doing the cooking.

'Why, we will cook ourselves,' I said, 'we've had enough practice.'

He seemed surprised and laughed a little, nervously, as he left.

*   *   *

That night we heard the green vapour rush along the valley. The temperature dropped suddenly and we turned our heating up and lit the first fire of the winter. In the morning the vapour was gone but the days were much cooler now and foam would squeeze from time to time. We were glad of our cosy house, but Henry had still not reappeared.

The first drum of Smolene we had purchased when we arrived on Provender was almost finished. When I had purchased it I naturally sought the best quality I could find but I had had no idea then that there was such a range of Smolene available. Every town seemed to blend its own from the numerous Smolene refineries dotted all over Provender. These in turn received Smolene of all grades from different Smolene wells, the grades varying according to the depth it was extracted from and the nature of the overlying rocks. The Smolene extracted from beneath the sea-bed is thin and almost clear, ideal for Hollombrost and Sprillet. Whereas the deeper reserves are thicker and darker and more suitable for food with a rich enough flavour to compete with the Smolene, such as Nullion or Cutling. Before purchasing our next drum we decided to visit a local Smolene blendery and choose for ourselves. We found the warehouse down a back street in Bepommel, near the market. The vendor, a Drisk, seemed to know all about us when we said where we lived.

'You are having a party?' he asked.

We said we were at the end of the year, and asked his advice on our choice of Smolene.

'What's it for?' he asked.

'For ourselves, mainly,' I said, 'and guests from time to time.'

'For yourselves?' he asked, laughing.

'Why, yes, of course.'

'Then it is true. Something subtle then, just a hint of after-taste and a tang of complimentary flavour. You want to go

142

down well with your guests, eh?' He laughed heartily and showed us the drum he recommended. He had blended it from fourteen different Smolenes and it made the very best of any food, he used it himself. We took the drum and left.

Henry turned up late one morning with Neville and some doors. They worked into the evening fitting doors and tidying up the damage from earlier visits. We had insisted on Trake boarding to cover up the Moostrin which glowed most disconcertingly at night and upset the ambience of the hover lights we had purchased through Constance and Deverell at great expense. These were the males of a species of fly that hovered in one spot and emitted a warm glow whenever it saw a supine female of the species. At a given sign from the female, an involuntary shudder, it would drop like a stone on to her and its light would go out. By leaving a small but anatomically accurate model of a female just under wherever you required light the fly would hover there all evening, feeding quietly on any Hully flies that it attracted.

Before he and Neville left Henry told us that the gratification suite was ready and, as the sound of the Zulex faded out along the track, we tiptoed up to look. The door was heavy and the bolt sturdy. We shut the door behind us and bolted it tightly. I switched it on to warm it up and was just reaching up to switch on the extractor fan when I overbalanced and sat down heavily on the radial arm, bending it. My wife and I looked at each other. We had only just had it repaired. I wondered how I would be able to face Mr Malvern and, in the meantime, our long-awaited suite was again inoperable. We returned downstairs in silence for a large snack.

When we arrived back from Bepommel with a few provisions we found Henry working upstairs in our bedroom, filling a hole in the ceiling he had just made with his boot. Every time it looked as if the work was almost finished something would happen to set it back even further. Alf and Don arrived with the Trake boarding for the ground floor and neatly swept a cluster of Hollombrost plaster off the ceiling. Neville hammered away in the ablution suite and a small chip of Trake flew up and chipped the Molar pan rim. It seemed impossible that we would ever have a finished house to ourselves, but we knew that it would happen one day. Then we would have the rest of our lives to learn all about our beloved Provender and share that knowledge with a few good friends with space enough for all our needs.

We were waiting once more for Henry to return after one of his customary short bursts of activity – he had caused more damage than he had repaired on the last visit – when Trevor arrived, loudly, in his ancient Stromba. It must have been at least a month since we called him and asked him to look at our Flasted 49. He stood on the edge of the lagoon and viewed it where it lay on the bottom, beneath the cold water.

'Too cold to go in now,' he said. We resisted the temptation to tell him how warm it had been a month earlier. 'I'll hook it out,' he said. We went indoors, well out of the way, and had a snack while we tried to ignore the sounds of Trevor's attempts. He tapped on the door some time later to tell us he had pulled it out but that he had snapped the bowsprit in the process. He said he would come back as soon as he could to repair the hole and mend the bowsprit and could he come to our party? We told him he could, if he had it properly fixed and finished in time. He seemed pleased and eager to comply. He was about to go when he stopped and looked as if he wanted to ask us something.

'Yes?' I said encouragingly.

'Well,' he said, then thought better of it.

'Go on.'

'Well, I just wondered what your taste was like.'

'Our taste is impeccable.' I laughed at the incongruity of the question. 'Surely you realize that all Conimunculi have excellent taste?'

'Oh. Terrific. Well, I'm looking forward to it.'

'Just get our Flasted 49 back in action.'

'You can count on it,' he said and then drowned out all sounds for the next ten minutes as he disappeared down the valley. We were left looking at the sad wreckage of our Flasted 49 on the patio. As he faded from hearing I heard our 'screen indoors and rushed in. It was an unsolicited call, someone had betrayed our code number. This was the first we had received on Provender. We knew it would not be the last now.

'Good day,' a small shrivelled creature, probably an Obling, screeched from the 'screen. 'We are opening a new branch of the Alien Alliance Bank on a planet near you. Why not open an account with us? We know your Credit Rating is B24 and that entitles you to our unique range of services.' I tried to turn the 'screen off but they must have used an override unit which operates once you accept the call. It was not possible to question the creature, the only option being to leave the room and wait until the message was finished. 'We offer competitive species ratings for Conimunculi drivers and . . .' I left the room. We would have to have our code changed now. No doubt countless other corporations were preparing to invade our privacy even at that moment.

I particularly objected to the Alien Alliance Bank. It started up new temporary branches all over the galaxy, persuaded creatures to open accounts with it at attractive introductory rates and then for the first year opened at such awkward hours that few creatures could ever get to it. Then it would close, citing lack of patronage by customers as the main reason, leaving them with their next branch so far away that most creatures' life spans were too short for the journey. We felt sure that the Galactic Bank should have put a stop to it years before if it had any claim to being the ultimate regulatory body. Instead, it got itself involved with ludicrous schemes purporting to be beneficial to the galaxy. It had sponsored the expedition that set off in search of the legendary 'Lost Library of Hick'. The fully automated satellite library had suffered a power surge and withdrew itself, spinning off into deep space. By the time it was tracked down it owed itself such an enormous sum in fines that it could not afford to take itself back. The expedition therefore concluded, after checking back with the Bank's accountants, that it was cheaper to leave it where it was. Perhaps its worst record of all has been with its Retarded Planet Rescue Plan. Their advisory panels consist entirely of accountants. For example, the problem with Gibble 8, an outer planet weaving an unpredictable orbit around the twin stars of Cuprix and Niblon, was deemed by the panel not to be its erratic climate, its thin soil or its depressingly stupid dominant race of sports-mad Tripeds, but its lack of borrowed funds. The panel decided that what was needed was a massive loan at three points above base rate. The Tripeds gratefully used it to build a massive sports complex on their only area of cultivable soil. The Bank encouraged them to hold an intergalactic clawball contest there and gave them the necessary additional finance at four points above base rate. The home planet's team lost and a post-match scuffle by opposing gangs of clawball vandals destroyed the sports complex, the planet's only Cosmodrome and every last remaining Triped.

I poked my head back into the room. The 'screen message had finished. I was about to leave when the screen whistled again. I removed its core.

DECEMBER

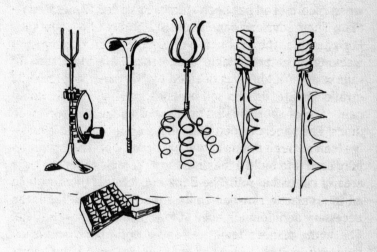

We had been thinking for quite some time that our newly extended, now almost finished house, required something more beyond mere furniture to make it a home. We needed to capture the essence of Provender and place it within our walls. The creatures of Provender regard food as their art form, there are few artists using any other media. Lesley's plasterwork was of course an artistic expression, as too were Henry's fireplaces and Neville's attempts to conceal some of George's surface pipework, but these were not art for art's sake. Constance and Deverell's multiplex was crammed with what they considered to be art, but it was too refined and artificial for our tastes. We wanted to find a Provender-born creature who lived and breathed art, who woke up in the morning and created because it had to, because it simply had no choice. I asked Henry, when next he visited to repair a repair, if he knew of any such artists. I thought he might be scornful of such ideas, but, in fact, he knew of just such an artist, a distant cousin of his, by chance, who lived in a hovel constructed of old Smolene drums and spent his waking hours trying to coax shapes out of lumps of Drib with a batterer. We asked for directions to find him.

'Oh, no visitors,' Henry said. 'He is a recluse, but I'm sure he will visit you if I ask him. Better be well before the end of the month though, eh?'

I told him that there was no real urgency, but bearing in mind the length of time it took for anything to happen on Provender, there was no harm in setting things in motion. We were surprised therefore to receive a visit from the artist the very next morning.

He was larger than Henry and clad entirely in black shiny skins with blobs of Drib all over them. He wore three black eye patches and a tame Pataguin sat on his shoulder and regarded his remaining eye with evident relish.

'You require the services of an artist?' he asked in perfect Coniman. We were taken aback.

'Let Rolf create for you,' the Pataguin shrieked, also in perfect Coniman. We were aghast. I had never heard a Pataguin speak. One is always put off eating anything that speaks.

'He only mimics,' the artist laughed in Spheraglese. We asked him in and offered him a Halmatrope and he sat down with a creaking sound, deep into a chair, and looked at us unblinkingly with his eye. Tudor crept slowly towards him, then disappeared at speed when he saw the Pataguin.

'We would like to commission a small work for our house,' I began.

'Small?' he said. 'What is begun must be finished, it may be small, it may not.'

'Ah, yes, but not too large, if that is at all possible?'

'Something for the fireplace? Or freestanding in the middle of a room?' he asked. Then his eye closed and he started to shake violently. The Pataguin took off and circled the room squawking, 'He's off again, he's off again,' in Spheraglese. When his eye opened he was calm.

'I saw it,' he said. 'It was the trail of the green vapour, twisting around the stripped stems of putrage where a Cutling suckled its young.'

'That sounds the sort of thing,' I said doubtfully. It sounded a complex undertaking to me. 'When could you finish it by?'

'A few days if you're pressed.'

'As quickly as that?' we marvelled.

'It will be conceptual you understand. I have to persuade the Drib how I feel. Then it responds.'

'Well, thank you then, Rolf. We look forward to seeing you and, and your creation.'

He strode off down the track, the Pataguin firmly back on his shoulder. A little later I was sure I caught the glint of a Ferenziculo vanishing fast down the track into the valley below.

We had decided to cancel all visits from guests until after the party. There were constant visits from our artisans, but still they seemed no nearer to completion. Henry would turn up to do a job and then discover he had left behind the appropriate tool. He would make things worse by trying to use an inappropriate tool and then not return for another two days. Trevor had managed to relaunch the Flasted 49 but it listed alarmingly. We told him it would not do. Lesley turned up in quite the wrong frame of mind to repair the delicate plaster ceiling and left a lifelike but quite unsuitable shape dangling just above the door for all to see.

We decided to leave them all to it. Perhaps our constant indignant vigilance was putting them off.

We therefore planned to visit an ancient Halmatrope cellar to buy some supplies for ourselves and for the party. The cellar was in the sole charge of an old Drool who had lost the use of his legs. It was built into the side of a hill and, once through the narrow entrance, the groined arches of the roof inside soared upwards and the walls were concealed entirely by rack upon rack of bottles. The old Drool presided over a small table with two chairs in the middle of the great room. He told us it had once been the debating chamber of the first Bepommel Council. The Councillors would be bricked in until they reached a unanimous decision. The quality of the Halmatrope would determine how quickly they were prepared to bury their differences and no problem was ever found that was too intractable to be solved by this method. It would no doubt have persisted until this day had it not been for a disastrous year of Halmatrope. The various opposing factions were unanimous in deciding that they all felt ill and that the proceedings should in future be carried out by some other method. Thus the chamber fell into disrepair until its reinstatement for the obvious purpose of Halmatrope storage. I perused the labels and climbed the ladder to make selections before placing them on the table before the old Drool. When we had finished he bade us take a seat.

'Ah, I can see you are a creature who knows his Halmatrope,' he said, with difficulty, raising himself on his elbows to speak.

'You have a fine selection here, sir,' I said, for it was indeed so.

'Tell me what you think of this,' he said, and brought a bottle and two glasses out from under the table. He wrang the contents expertly into each glass so that there was not a bubble or trace of sediment. My wife and I each took a sip. It was as if something had grabbed our tongues and refused to let go. The Drool chuckled at our reactions. Drools had no such problems with their single purpose food vacuoles. One by one it played upon our tastebuds then in harmonic groups, each time gaining in intensity, finally arching into a shuddering crescendo as the last drop slid down our throats, our tongues collapsed exhausted back behind our teeth, totally lifeless.

'You want some more?' the old Drool laughed. I found it impossible to articulate and shook my head. Some things are just too good. We paid and took away our purchases, my wife managing a very passable attempt at thanking him in Drool, but it was a full hour before our tongues returned to normal. This made it difficult for us to express ourselves when we returned home to find Rolf with his creation in the back of Henry's Zulex. It was indeed at first view startling, some might say, horrific. Rolf must have believed it had rendered us speechless for we were unable to actually say anything until Rolf, Henry and the two cousins had carried it through into our living room. It was larger than we had anticipated, but one had to admire the sheer physical ability of the artist to so transform such an unexciting substance as Drib.

'Like it, eh?' Rolf beamed, when it was placed right in the middle of our room. My tongue was returning to life, but I only felt confident enough to say 'Mmm'. We realized that a true work of art needs to be lived with and experienced on many levels over a period of time before any real judgements can be made. I did not, however, feel that constantly bumping into it was necessary for its appreciation. I managed to ask them to move it as far into a corner as it would go.

'Too much for you, eh?' Rolf grinned. I thought it best just to splutter my agreement. Rolf slapped me consolingly on the back. 'You'll get used to it.' Then he handed me his bill. That took some getting used to. 'No hurry,' he said, 'long as it's before your party, eh?' Then he laughed and the Pataguin laughed too. I paid him and he was gone before our powers of speech returned fully.

With two days to go before our party Henry and his cousins arrived early, determined that when they left the job would be pronounced finished. They tiptoed so delicately around the house taking such care to avoid having to repair repairs to repairs that when they finally presented themselves to us to give us the good news we did not have the heart to mention the few last blemishes they had overlooked. They were about to leave when my wife asked them to tap a hook in the wall to hang a Flora Diraea 'Summer Plague' rug on. The hook unfortunately pierced one of George's pipes which lay just below the surface of the plaster. A thin stream of hot purple fluid sprang out across the room. Henry covered it with his cap and I rushed to 'screen George.

Miraculously enough, George was in and he appreciated that there was an element of urgency in my request for help.

153

None the less, Henry was beginning to tire when George arrived with his toolkit. He passed Rolf's creation in the living room and observed, 'Oh, I see Rolf's sold you one of his crashed Stromba chassis too, has he?' much to my annoyance, having just paid Rolf. George plugged the hole in the pipe and gave Henry a withering look. We saw them all off and said we would see them at the party.

We were overjoyed. Everything was as finished as it would ever be, the house was ours again, all ours. The next day we knew we would be moving furniture, purchasing provisions and preparing for the following day's party, so we determined to relax with a large snack and a Halmatrope and just enjoy the peace. We deserved a rest after all the work of the year. We looked back and reminisced. We talked of all the delicious food, all the delightful drinks and all the wonderful creatures who had welcomed us to their planet so warmly. I thanked my wife for the wonderful present she gave me when we first moved into our house. This tiny Wordpack on which I have been compiling this diary since the beginning of the year has scarcely left my palm. I have become so used to the simple tendril-tip controls that I can add extra snippets to it almost without thinking. I am not sure what I will do with it at the end of this, our first complete calendar year. Perhaps I will just keep on year after year recording each delightful event.

When we arrived back from our second trip to Bepommel laden with more provisions for our party we discovered Henry, George and Trevor waiting for us. They were neatly dressed, not in their working clothes and each one held an envelope which he handed to me. They were, as I suspected, final bills. I pointedly looked across at the Flasted 49 when I took Trevor's. It was sitting neatly in the water, the bowsprit would never be the same again but he seemed to have solved the listing problem. We asked them in. They seemed very serious. I realized that they thought that to have everything finished before the party was a two-sided affair. They had finished their part, now we had to finish ours and pay them. Adopting their tone, I solemnly paid them before offering them a drink. They brightened up.

'We thought we ought to settle everything before the party,' George explained. 'There may not be an opportunity otherwise.'

'Quite, quite,' I nodded. 'We understand.' We lifted our glasses and toasted their good health. They drank up and prepared to leave. George looked a little awkward and asked, 'About tomorrow, what sort of time?'

'If you all turn up about midday, George, and then it can go on as long as you want.'

George still looked awkward. 'And you? What time shall we . . .?' He was not his usual self at all.

'Listen, George,' I said, trying to put him at ease – he had probably heard what formal affairs Conimunculi parties could be, 'We just want you all to have a good time, don't mind us, eat as much as you can. We don't want anything left at the end.' That seemed to put his mind at rest. They all shook our palms firmly and departed.

We woke early. The weather was kind to us on our party day. It was cool, but not cold, with no foam to be seen anywhere in the clear sky. A slight breeze rippled the lagoon waters and we ate a hearty breakfast and ran over our plans for a busy morning of preparation and cooking. Tudor curled in and out around us and we fed him little scraps. We knew it was naughty to encourage him but it would be his party day too.

Just before midday, with the tables and all available surfaces groaning under the weight of our party provisions, we got changed ready for our guests.

We could hear the approaching vehicles long before we saw any of them. The first in the line was Trevor and his wife. He held up everyone behind him so that by the time he reached us in his old Stromba, Henry, George and their respective wives were only just behind. They were in their very best clothes as far as we could see, and Henry was in a Stromba, not his old Zulex. We invited them all in and handed round the Halmatrope. Lesley wiggled in with her swaggering partner, Beverley. They seemed too intent on each other to bother anyone else.

Alf arrived with his little wife and also the Spansule driver who had delivered some of our materials. We were handing round second Halmatropes to the earlier guests when Neville and his old mother appeared. She was extremely small and withered. I made a personal note not to confuse her with the grilled Nullion later on in the day. We urged everybody to help themselves to the enormous piles of food we had prepared but they seemed strangely reluctant to fill themselves. They took little helpings just to please us, we suspected. Obviously, they would eat in earnest later, when the party was in full swing. Guests started to appear who we only vaguely recognized and had not actually invited. Creatures from the shops and markets in Bepommel and waiters and waitresses I recognized from the restaurants we had eaten in. We welcomed them all, the more the merrier. It was wonderful.

Then Don slipped in, he must have only just arrived. He whispered in Henry's ear. Henry stamped on the floor twice to silence everyone.

'Ah,' Henry said to my wife and me, 'I think we might have a little problem. You'd best come outside.' We followed Henry out and everybody followed us. There, outside was Henry's Zulex with something enormous on the back, covered in a sheet. Mr Dobson was leaning against it, grinning.

'What is it?' I asked.

'It's for you,' Henry said. 'From all of us.' He pulled back the sheet. '. . . A Conimunculi cooker!'

'Good gracious, what a marvellous find, but where will we put it?' I said, looking at my wife.

She looked alarmed. When I turned back they were all advancing on us with open mouths.

'Oh.' I said. 'I see.'

THE END